ONE

There was a time when a strange noise in the dead of night would have jerked Louis Cooke awake in a flash. He thought he was past that time, the old life, the former him, but his eyes snapped open and he was on his feet immediately.

3am. A noise outside the house. Great.

The noise repeated: a scratching sound, like a cat trying to get in the building. They had no cat. He looked at his wife, who was softly snoring in the middle of the bed.

When the sound came a third time, Louis exited the bedroom and headed down the stairs. Their bedroom was at the back of the house, so whatever had made the sound was in the rear yard. He headed into the kitchen just in time to hear the same scraping sound. What he hoped was a cat was at the back door.

The cat theory popped like a balloon when he heard the squeak of the door handle. The blinds were closed, so he couldn't see outside. His first thought was to shout out, to scare away the burglar. But then that long-dormant part of him chose another path, and he left the room.

He quietly unlocked the front door and, barefoot and in just boxer shorts, stepped out. He darted around the side of the house. The driveway was barred by a low wooden fence, which the kids loved to use as a tennis net. He stepped over without breaking stride and approached the back corner of the building.

He moved his head slowly, exposing the backyard an inch at a time. Until he saw the intruder. Absolutely not a damn cat.

A tall man in black and wearing a balaclava was standing at the door, using a crowbar to try to gain entry. Louis felt his pulse race. A strange man wanted into the house, where Louis's kids and wife slept in peace. Maybe he wanted goods to sell for drugs. But maybe he wanted blood.

First option: police. But an inner voice overruled that decision.

The side of the house was bordered by a thin strip of decorative stones. Louis grabbed one and lobbed it. It sailed past the intruder and hit the wooden fence. As planned, the man in black forgot his mission for a moment and turned towards the sound. It put his back to Louis, and he was on it a second later, one arm around the thief's neck. Louis locked in a move called a rear-naked choke.

The intruder said, 'You've lived this...' and no more.

Louis tightened the choke and the remaining words turned into a gurgle. He kicked the scumbag's legs out, dropping him hard onto his arse on the paving slabs. Two hands dug into Louis's forearm to try to break the stranglehold, but Louis vetoed that escape plan. He stuck with his own scheme to strangle this bastard asleep and let him awake to an audience of police officers.

But then, despite the darkness, he got a good look at the fingers attempting to remove his arm. On all five, between the first and middle knuckles, was a tattoo of a little black dagger.

Shocked, Louis loosened his choke.

THE PACT

ALEX ROSE

BLOODHOUND
BOOKS

www.bloodhoundbooks.com

Print ISBN: 978-1-917449-8-16

PART 1

TWO

Louis entered the living room with a tall glass of water. He held out the drink. A four-fingered hand took it and the intruder sat back in the armchair.

'Nice place,' the man said. He'd now taken off his balaclava to expose a grimy brown beard and a buzzcut the same colour. 'How you pay for all this? What you do now?'

Louis sat on the sofa. 'I work security.'

'Seems to pay well. I see a wedding photo, so you got married.'

'I did.'

'And some toys. So you had kids.'

'I did.'

The man drank heavily. 'I get you're still a bit knocked for six. But come on. How many kids? Names?'

'Theo and Louise. They're eight. Twins.'

'What's the wife like? Wild in bed?'

Louise sighed. 'You don't look too healthy, Owen. Let me say a one-word guess, and don't be offended. Drugs?'

He looked offended. 'I'm still fit, man. Maybe I look older

than I should. Whatever. No one's a saint. Not happy to see your old pal?'

'Sure, if I'd bumped into you down the pub. But not after you tried to crowbar your way into my house in the dead of night.'

Owen finished his drink and started lobbing the glass from one hand to the other. 'I wasn't trying to break in. Well, not quite. I wasn't out robbing houses. I knew this was your pad. I came to see you.'

'Next time, knock on the door on a sunny afternoon. What the hell was all that about?'

'Just testing you to see if you still had it. The skills, man. Each of us an army of one, eh? Seems you lost nothing. My neck still hurts.'

Louis heard a creak from upstairs and looked at the ceiling. He prayed it was the house settling and not his wife waking. 'That was another life, Owen. These days I'm a world champion washing machine loader. I've mastered the art of driveway weeding.'

'Muscle memory, old pal. Like breathing.'

'I'm not sure that's one. But let's get back to why you're here. Are you after money? Don't let the house fool you. We're struggling with the mortgage and haven't had a holiday in ages. We've got two cars but one's dead. I just had to cancel the kids' gymnastics because we can't afford it. Don't ask me for a handout or a loan. I can't help.'

Owen placed his empty glass on its side on the coffee table. It started to roll to the edge, and Louis caught it when it fell off. 'Why's that table warped?' Owen said.

'It's fine. It's the floor that's not level.' He stood. It was a hint that it was time for his guest to leave. But Owen didn't move. He extracted a slip of paper from his pocket and held it out. Louis didn't take it, but he saw what was written in pen. A postcode. 'What's that?'

Owen put the paper on the arm of the chair and got up. 'Meet me there at seven tomorrow night. And I guarantee you'll be glad you did. I'm not going to say any more until then.'

'Saturday night? Can't mate. Me and the wife have something planned.'

Owen looked puzzled for a moment, then the penny dropped. 'No, tonight. My bad. I forgot–'

'Forgot it was three in the morning, right?'

He shrugged. 'I live a nocturnal life. So you'll come?'

Louis told Owen to stand up. When he did, Louis stepped closer, so their faces were just inches apart. 'Stare right into my eyes, Owen. I'm going to ask you a question.'

Owen laughed. 'You say another life, but now you reckon you can still tell when I'm lying?' Owen leaned close to Louis. 'Eyes locked. Face relaxed. Go for it.'

'Did you come here because you knew you could spin some bullshit about wanting to see your old pal? If you got caught robbing the place.'

Owen looked hurt by the accusation. 'We once trusted each other to the core, Louis. Now this?'

'Another life, Owen.'

Owen walked past Louis, headed for the door. Louis felt a pang of guilt at having suggested his one-time friend might have been here to steal. He called his name. Owen turned.

'I'll come, Owen. Seven tonight. Of course I will.'

'Good man. And for your information, I never planned to get into the house. The door's crappy wood. Crowbar would have got me through in two seconds. I made noise on purpose to get you downstairs. See what you'd do. And you did well. Army of one.'

'Goodnight, Owen.'

Louis held out a hand and Owen shook it. He walked his friend to the front door and locked it behind him.

When he returned to the bedroom, Sonia was still asleep in the middle of the bed. He got in beside her and stared at the ceiling. The dark and the silence emphasised the buzz he still felt in his muscles. Owen hadn't been as off the mark as Louis had suggested. Despite believing the house was about to be burgled, he hadn't felt fear. And, if he was honest with himself, part of him had enjoyed sneaking through the dark to take down an enemy.

THREE

Two hours after he'd left Louis's house in Hounslow, Owen was back east in Tower Hamlets. It was still dark, but parts of the city were stirring awake. He chained his pushbike to a lamppost outside Cemetery Park and headed inside.

His mother used to bring him here as a kid when she visited her grandfather's burial site, so he knew the place like the back of his hand. There were pathways where old graves lurked amongst the trees on both sides and he always stuck to the dead centre of the track so zombies couldn't whip out hands to grab him. That silly fear was gone, but in the dark this place was still unnerving.

Not to all, though. Dead First World War soldiers had descendants who continued to mourn, and it was these people who provided for him. He hung around for an hour and then got lucky. Along came a guy who looked old enough to have been in the trenches with whoever he lost.

Owen followed him for ten minutes, until the old lad stepped off the path and stomped through the undergrowth. He stopped at a battered old headstone shaped like a cross, although it was tilted far to one side and now resembled an X.

Owen made his move. 'I lost my train fare,' he said. He was just ten feet behind the old man, who wore an ancient brown corduroy suit. There was no response, so Owen repeated his line with extra volume.

The man turned from the grave. He looked annoyed to have company. 'What's that, sonny?'

'I need money to get back to Scotland to see my mother before she dies. She's in a hospice.'

The old guy flicked a hand dismissively and turned back to the grave. Oh well. The lie had never worked.

Owen stepped up and between the man and the grave. In his hand was a large screwdriver with duct tape around the handle. As well as the weapon, he'd brought a cool prepared line. 'All your cash right now, or there will be two bodies here.'

Some old farts didn't like technology and carried cash. This one had a wallet busting with it. Jackpot. His pocket weighed down, Owen scarpered for his bike. Once mounted on it, he raced a mile from the hot zone before pausing to count his loot. Ninety quid. Enough for Sally and then some.

Sally's bedsit was above a grocer's in Stepney, just a quick ride west. He was there by six, which was too early. He hung around and played on his phone for an hour, until he saw the curtains open. He headed round back and climbed a set of iron stairs and knocked on the door at the top.

'Who's there?' Sally called through the door a minute later. He gave his name and she opened up.

She was in a tacky outfit that added a decade to her twenty-four years, had a nose as uneven as a bad boxer's, and sported a tight blonde perm that went out of fashion years ago. But one man's meat is another man's poison, and to him she was beautiful. 'Busy?' he said.

'I might be.'

He waved a £20 note under her nose. 'Busy?'

'I am now.' She took the cash, made it disappear, and led him inside.

As always, the sex was fantastic. Sally gave value for money, although he didn't like to dwell on how she'd developed such bedroom skills. She'd given deathbed memories to men whose faces she'd forgotten and there had to be plenty who'd promised they could whisk her away into a better life.

Owen had been guilty of the same, but unlike all the others, his words hadn't been pillow talk. Unbeknownst to her, she had found in him a gem amongst rocks. Today she'd learn that. He'd waited months for this moment.

He chose it carefully. After the sex, she got showered and redressed and, as always, told him she had things to attend to. It was her standard line and equated to: *get lost*. This time he didn't bounce up and leave. He lay right there on the bed and said, 'What if I said I could take you out of this life?'

She was at her dressing table, reapplying lipstick after leaving a mass of it on his dick. She didn't even look at him. 'Plenty have said that to me, darling.'

'I mean it, though.'

'I've got a rich regular who said that. I even turned him down.'

'I've got a bunch of money coming. I can set us up.'

So much for the rich regular. She turned to him. 'How much? What are you offering me?'

'I've got over three grand coming on Sunday.'

She laughed and continued applying make-up. 'That's not a lot, baby. Maybe to you. I make that in a month sometimes. Once I did it in a day.'

He pretended she hadn't said that, but couldn't help wondering how she'd amassed such a payday. One wealthy client, or myriad? 'I have a business idea and it's gonna make me lots. I can take care of you.'

Finished sprucing herself up, she stood. 'I have to ask you to leave now, Owen. We'll see each other again soon. I've got another man coming in a bit.'

The door rocked in its frame as heavy fists knocked three times. So, she hadn't lied about another client. Owen got up. He extracted another £20 from his pocket and lobbed it on the bed. 'I'll cancel him.'

He went to the door to do just that.

'Moore?' said the shorter and younger of the three men standing outside. He was dressed in jeans and a camel jacket over a blue shirt, all thrown into mismatch by a beanie hat that hid his hair. 'Wow. Two birds with one stone.'

Sam. Shit. Owen tried to think fast, but got no time. One of the two others, both of whom were big men packed into tracksuits, grabbed Owen by the neck. The second took a fistful of hair. They marched him backwards and threw him on the bed. Sam entered and kicked the door shut behind him.

'Sam?' Sally said. 'I thought you were coming this afternoon.'

Sam approached her and held out a hand. Sally got a glass jar from a drawer in her dressing table and handed over the contents. A few hundred pounds, Owen figured. Sam pocketed it. 'Did you just fuck this guy? Did he pay?'

'Yes. I put the money in the jar.'

Sam turned to Owen. Now all three men hovered over him. 'That's a problem. Because this sleazeball shouldn't have money to spend like that. Because he has a dope habit and he owes someone. Know who?'

She said, 'You?'

'Yes. Me. Two hundred quid that he said he needed until Sunday to pay. So, Owen, I hope you can prove you have extra funds for shagging one of my lasses.'

'He says he has three and a bit grand coming on Sunday,' Sally piped up. Owen cursed aloud before he could stop it.

Sam smiled. 'Excellent news. Three grand? Is that right, Moore?'

Owen was well acquainted with this asshole and his foibles. If he didn't admit he had cash coming, Sam would decide that someone was lying. He'd have his goons smack them both around. Owen had no choice other than to come clean.

'Nice,' Sam said. 'But here's the problem, Moore. I can wait for what you owe. And I don't care if you bang my girls. This one here is my special girl, though. My girlfriend, actually. I only go for girls who can blow men's minds. I want my punters to have a good time, not have their minds blown. Not for such a low price. It's a thousand to have your mind blown. Did she blow your mind? I'll believe you either way.'

Again, this dickhead and his petty tricks. If Owen said Sally had blown his mind, he'd owe an extra thousand pounds. If he went the other way, well, wasn't that just a terrible insult against a man's 'girlfriend'? No choice. 'Yes, she did.'

'I guess that's a grand, then. I'll send a man to your mum's gaff on Sunday night. I think that's a good idea. No?'

It didn't matter if a police marching band was slated to play at his mum's house on Sunday evening. If he didn't agree, he would be accusing Sam of having a bad idea. That itself was a bad idea. The wannabe gangster was like a bar-room thug just waiting for someone to spill his pint so he could attack. For the third time Owen had to play along.

'Sure, Sam. That's a very good idea. Sunday night at my mum's house. A thousand pounds.'

Sam nodded. 'My men go in and out they come with a grand or a grand's worth, you understand?'

He did. If Owen wasn't there, Sam's bozos would take his

mother's property, and they wouldn't be polite and gentle about it. Owen promised he'd be there.

Sam seemed itching for more. He wanted to have someone hurt. Luckily, he gave it up. 'Now get out and let me have a word with my girlfriend.'

This part burned the most. Owen didn't want to leave Sally alone with her pimp. He wasn't sure if the bastard planned to hurt or fuck her. And he wasn't sure which was worse.

FOUR

Owen Moore had once been like a brother to Louis, but the passage of years was impossible to ignore. The guy he'd known way back hadn't been into drugs or burglaries. The new Owen was an unknown quantity, and that made it tough to fully trust him.

So, Louis drove to the meeting place early, and he watched his mirrors for a tail. The location was a pub in Finsbury Park bizarrely called The Shadow Realm. A real rough dive, given the mass of yobbos smoking out front and the souped-up boy rides in the car park. Louis parked his own vehicle in a remote corner and watched the building for a few minutes.

People came and went. He didn't see Owen arrive. He didn't see anyone who showed an interest in his vehicle. Maybe he was being paranoid.

At seven, he locked the car and headed into the pub. As soon as he entered the bustling lounge, he saw a table with two men at it. One was Owen. The second man was black and wore a sharp suit. The latter spotted Louis and yelled his name. There was instantly something familiar about the stranger. Now

Owen looked his way and waved. And then it dawned. Louis rushed over. The three men collided in a mass-hug. They softly headbutted each other. They yanked aside jumpers, jackets and shirts to expose the same left-shoulder tattoo – a black dagger in a green square, denoting the badge of 3 Commando Brigade. They were loud and the whole pub saw the show.

The three men sat. A pint of lager was already on the table for Louis. He was still half in disbelief. Owen Moore and Newton Meecham. His old army pals. 'I feel stupid for worrying that Owen was planning to set me up,' he said.

Newton said, 'I did the same after he jumped me on a golf course.'

Louis almost spat out his drink. 'Wait, you got jumped as well?'

Their stories poured out. Newton was now a restaurant owner and yuppie-type (minus the youth aspect) who liked to golf with his boring executive friends. Back when he'd served in the army, he'd had a loving wife and a mortgage. Now she was a sour ex who lived in his former house – a gift from him for their happy years – with another man.

Yesterday evening, he'd hit a sand trap on the fifth hole and Owen had jumped him from behind and said, 'You've lived this life long enough.'

Louis told Newton that he was married and with twins. He was a security guard in a shopping centre, where Sonia also worked in a store. He told his story briefly, 'Owen tried to get the jump on me with a faux burglary, but I turned the tables.' He got a high-five from Newton for a job well done. Attacking a guy at his home was maybe overstepping the line.

But Owen kept quiet about his time since their service days. It wasn't a great leap to assume he had nothing much to brag about. His refusal to say anymore more than, 'I spin some plates, don't you all worry,' left a silence that Newton used to steer the conversation to a more important subject.

'So why are we here?'

'This,' Owen said. He finished his pint of lager, turned, and lobbed the glass at the pool table, where it shattered on the baize to the angry surprise of a bunch of youngsters in mid-game.

FIVE

As one, the group of lads turned to face the source of the beer glass. Every table was taken, but there was no doubt who'd launched the missile. Not when Owen stood up and yelled, 'Foul shot, bozos.'

'Someone's in for a bruising,' one of the guys yelled. 'We'll go easiest on whoever's first. Come on, you bastards. Who's got balls?'

Owen put up a hand, as if to seek permission to speak. 'Your mum, according to all the guys round her estate.'

Speaking of balls, another of the young men grabbed one off the pool table and pitched it towards the enemy. Newton's chair was closest, so he felt the most vulnerable. He put up a defensive hand and the ball thudded into his palm and dropped to the floor. It looked like a neatly choreographed move from a Hollywood action flick.

But it was all good fortune and Newton knew it. His hand also damn hurt. In an equally flashy move, he stood, grabbed the back of his wooden chair, pivoted, and launched it. The chair hit the pitcher in the legs and sliced him down.

After that, another Hollywood-like scene erupted: a bar-room brawl.

Peaceful patrons fled. The staff dialled a trio of nines and screamed for ceasefire. Eight men in their twenties descended on three blokes in their early forties.

Still closest to the mob, Newton dropped the first two attackers with a parallel pair of hard jabs – the most cinematic moment yet.

Owen levelled down and grabbed an assailant around the waist, hoisted him up and dropped him hard onto his back.

Newton splashed his drink into the face of a floppy-haired man coming like a train. Blinded, the man couldn't defend against a fist fired at his gut.

Louis wanted no part of this melee and grabbed the closest guy. He got against the man's back in his second rear-naked choke of the day. On one side of him, Owen grabbed an aggressor's ears and dragged his face downward, into a rising knee. Newton, still in missile mode, skimmed a beermat at someone's face and it disoriented him enough to catch a follow-up jab to the eyes.

Louis kept hold of his catch. His intention was to hug the fool until this lark was all over. But then he saw someone extract a blade. Louis tripped his victim and stepped towards the knifeman. A powerful front kick to the chest knocked the man backwards, into a fallen comrade. He tripped and fell on his ass against the wooden bar wall.

Before he could even think of getting up, Louis stepped in, placed both hands atop the bar, and drove a knee into the man's face. The impact of the man's head into the bar wall shook peanuts in a bowl.

Louis then bent down and twisted the man's knife hand to release the weapon, which he kicked away. He grabbed the thug's hair. 'That's not in the Queensbury Rules.' He stood and kneed the bastard again, this time in the nose.

Hands grabbed him. He turned, a fist raised and ready, but it was Newton who stood there. 'Leaving time,' he yelled, then pulled Louis towards the door.

'Same time next week, fellas,' Owen shouted as they bolted. The set piece concluded with a comical moment as the three old friends hit the single doorway at the same time and got stuck in a tangle of limbs. They burst into the car park a few seconds later.

'My car,' Newton bellowed. He veered off at an angle and the others followed. As they bore down on a sleek grey Mercedes EQS with a big sticker – fōda – on the flank, Newton pressed a button on his fob and the driver's door started to open. Louis and Owen, who were fastest, got there first and yanked open the back doors. Newton leaped behind the wheel.

By this time a mob of angry and hurt young men had hit the car park and were thundering towards the Merc. 'No wheelspin. Bloody ABS,' Newton said as he threw the car at the exit. As it blew out and onto the road, a pool ball hit the back window and skidded off the angled glass.

'What the hell was that, Owen?' Louis said as the car fled the scene. 'Some of those dickheads might know where I work.'

'Well, they'll definitely know where I work because my restaurant name is on the side of this car.'

'Why'd you bring the sticker?' Owen said.

'Because I didn't expect a battle. I'll have a bloodthirsty mob invading the place. And they've seen my number plate.'

'Why'd you bring the plate?'

The sincerity in Owen's tone made Newton laugh. Louis copied. All three men had a guffaw.

'Seriously, though,' Louis said. 'What was all that for?'

Owen slapped backs. 'Just a test, boys, and you all passed. We've still got the skills. Armies of one. I think you're all ready for what I got planned.'

SIX

Newton made innumerable turns just in case their enemies had continued the chase in vehicles. Once certain nobody was on their tail, he stopped in the rear car park of a closed bank. He turned to Owen.

'Okay, we're safe. So now start explaining.'

All eyes were on him. 'What I said to each of you. "You've lived this life long enough." Who's–'

'You didn't say that to me,' Louis said. 'Remember why that was?'

Owen gave him the finger. 'So, who's bored of the dullness?'

They were looking at him funny. Newton said, 'This life? What's that mean?'

'I reckon Owen has joined a suicide cult.' Louis again. 'No thanks, pal.'

Another finger from Owen. 'Look what we got here. A guy who sells dead pigs. A guy who chases kids out of shops. That anyone's big dream when we got out of the army?'

'Hey, I like my life, Owen,' Louis said. 'I got a wife and kids and the job pays well. It's fun. What are you talking about? Are you saying we should go spice up our lives with some bar-room brawls?'

'Don't you all miss the old life? I'm offering a chance to get it back.' He could tell he was only causing more confusion. 'Why did we join the army? You, Newton, you told me you like thrills. You joined up for the danger.'

Newton shrugged.

'Not me,' Louis said. 'I was young and confused.'

'But you were fearless. First in the door. Last to leave a hot zone. And you were always a sarcastic knobhead. You obviously kept that bit.'

Before Louis could offer a comeback, Newton said, 'Just cut to the chase, Owen. You arranged for all us to meet because you said you had a proposition. I'm not sure I'd like to hear it, but go for it anyway.'

'Okay. So, you guys wanna earn ten thousand pounds for a day's danger and combat?'

'I earn that in a week, pal,' Newton said.

'That a no? From anyone? Guys, if you don't even want to hear it, say so. Anyone not game can get out of the car right now.'

Newton laughed. 'It's my car.'

'Then I'll go. Nice knowing you, guys.'

Glances were exchanged. Newton locked the car doors. Owen could have still opened his, but the message had been given. Nobody wanted to back out just yet.

'Good move, guys,' Owen said. 'So, let me tell you a story...'

SEVEN

The main theme of any gang is comradeship and loyalty and The Ninja Warriors thrived because of this. Local yobs with nothing better to do joined because they liked to cause trouble. Others enter the ranks for the brotherhood. Some liked the protection it offered. A few enjoyed the power that came with calling yourself a gangster.

It all sounded imposing, but The Ninja Warriors wasn't a hardcore gang with clout and respect. A noun more used often than any other was 'nuisance'. Out in the big, bad world, this collection of annoying little teenagers and early twentysomethings wouldn't have made a dent. It was a different story on tiny Parry Estate in Ickenham.

The residents of the estate lived in fear. There was no major crime, but petty infractions were a daily problem. 'Chinese water torture,' as one resident put it. Kids would piss against houses. They'd yell at local girls. They'd feed dogshit through letterboxes. They'd squirt superglue into door locks. That and so much more.

One day somebody had yelled at a thug for leaning on his

car. The next morning he found all four of his tyres slashed. The day after that, his front door handle was sawn off while he was at work. He was hounded for months, until he could take no more and sold his house way below its meagre worth. The residents quickly learned to avoid reprimanding the Warriors, lest a bullseye was painted on your face.

Close to RAF Northolt, Parry Estate was a tight knot of streets surrounded by fields on three sides and with only a single road in or out. On that road was a bus stop, where a spotter would be stationed to watch for cops. If he spotted any, he'd make a call and hang up after one ring.

But that ring was a signal to the rest of his gang. By the time police arrived, the thugs would be long gone. This had happened so often that the police had given up responding to calls.

So, the residents gritted their teeth and endured the torture. They plastered CCTV cameras on their walls, hoping to capture evidence of serious crimes that might interest law enforcement. But as the cameras went up, hoodies and scarves and sunglasses became the new lout fashion. Air rifles took out the cameras that the thugs couldn't steal.

Then came what some residents called Chernobyl Night. On Tuesday, well after midnight, the residents of Main Street were woken by serious banging on their doors. For once it wasn't the Warriors larking about. Cops and firemen were everywhere, ordering people out of their homes.

The estate's sole corner shop had a flat above it, whose resident got use of the yard out back. That resident was the leader of the Warriors, a man who called himself The Ginger Ninja. He and his cronies used the back yard to make a quick buck by offering car welding services. For that they needed acetylene gas bottles and had a stack in the shed.

The Warriors had their own enemies beyond the estate, and on that Tuesday someone they'd wronged chose payback. He sneaked into the yard, opened the shed, and squirted lighter fluid everywhere. Someone spotted the flames and called it in. Worried about a mighty explosion, the authorities evacuated the entire street.

Some residents had to get hotels, while others were housed a couple of miles away in a school gym, bedding down in sleeping bags. A newspaper article described the scene as like something from a war-torn country.

Chernobyl Night was the turning point. The residents had had enough and something had to be done. The first step was taken by a lady whose son was an amateur boxer living in America. When he came to visit on Wednesday morning, after the residents had been allowed back home, she told him the story.

'Someone needs to clip these assholes round the ear,' he said. 'Kids like that need terrorising to learn the error of their ways.'

She liked the idea. And her son was a tough boxer. 'Can't you do it?' she asked him.

He gave it a shot. A couple of teenagers were hanging round his BMW, so he headed out and told them to clear off. They obeyed, but later he found all four tyres popped. He told his mum: 'I shouldn't have done that. Now they might hassle you. They need a bigger threat.'

'Don't you have boxer friends?'

'Yeah, in New York. They can't help.'

His mother spoke to a friend, whose son played football for a local amateur team. Including substitutes, he probably knew twenty men. But when asked to help, he said his pals were sportsmen, not soldiers.

Soldiers. The two women immediately thought of Ms Moore because her boy, Owen, was a former commando. They made a call and Ms Moore relayed their query to her son.

'Sure,' Owen said. 'I know some tough guys. They can whip the arses of a bunch of idiots. But they'll want paying.'

EIGHT

'Wait a minute,' Newton said when Owen had finished his story. 'That's your great plan? For us to go fight a gang of thugs?'

'So you acknowledge it's great?' Owen responded.

'And your mum is going to pay us ten thousand pounds?'

Owen laughed. 'My ma didn't put the cash up. Word got around. The residents liked it. They had a whip round.'

Louis could hardly believe it. 'A bunch of people on the estate chipped in money and now there's ten thousand pounds? How many people?'

'I dunno. Nine or ten or so. It's worth it to them. If they can get rid of these idiots for good.'

'And so you turned to us? Did you mention that these army guys you know are now working, middle-aged men with families and jobs?'

'The fire's still in you boys. And the skills. We just saw that. One night's work, fellas. Tomorrow. Ten grand for a bit of long-missed action.'

'Dangerous. Mad.'

'Silly A-Team bullshit.'

Owen said, 'All of the above, lads. Mad, dangerous, silly A-Team bullcrap. But it's real, and the peeps are waiting for an answer. So who's a superhero, and who's a pussy?'

NINE

They gave it an hour before heading back to The Shadow Realm pub for Louis's car. Newton dumped his friends on a nearby street so his vehicle wouldn't be spotted by the enemy. They swapped mobile phone numbers.

'We'll call you if we get killed,' Louis said.

Newton gave a thumbs-up and departed. Louis and Owen walked around the corner, then paused to watch the activity outside the pub. Still there were young drinkers in the beer garden, but nobody they recognised from the mob they'd offended. Owen headed into the hot zone first. Louis watched him sneak to a tree near the back fence, unlock his pushbike, and pedal away.

Louis's turn. He bolted into the car park and jumped into his ride, and got it out of there. Nice and easy. It was not yet 10pm.

Louis tried to get his head around the last couple of hours, and the job Owen had presented to them – which he'd called Operation Kickass. Newton had signed up without pause. Money wasn't a factor, which left only a motive Owen had hinted at: the thrill.

Newton had admitted as much by moaning about the cushioned lifestyle of an executive. He played golf and attended business functions and everybody he knew was boring. He yearned for action.

Louis was the dissenting voice. He was all for helping the vulnerable, but not via the proposed method. They would be taking the law into their own hands, which would make them criminals. His fear wasn't getting harmed, but being arrested. If he got a conviction, he'd lose his job.

'So you're out?' Newton had asked back in the car.

Louis had paused. The 'operation' alone didn't interest him. He didn't need the hassle. The money did appeal, however. A third of ten thousand pounds was sorely needed in his household.

'I'll think about it,' he'd said. 'I'll call you tomorrow morning with my answer.'

He could not make the decision alone. He had to ask his wife. Sonia would look past the money and she was a good soul. If she thought his playing vigilante wasn't immoral, then he'd join his friends tomorrow night. His worry wasn't just her answer, though. If she was dead against the 'Operation', then the very fact that he'd considered it would upset her.

Because of this, he said nothing when he got home.

'How did it go?' she asked. She was watching TV on the sofa, legs hidden under a blanket, glass of wine in her hand. The bottle on the coffee table was empty.

That morning, he'd told her about Owen. Unable to lie and unwilling to worry her with a burglary story, he'd said that his old Navy comrade had 'contacted' him late last night and arranged a drink at a pub.

She was eager for details of that meeting, so he gave them. She was delighted to hear that another of his old friends had attended. He couldn't lie, but he could omit, so she learned nothing about the bar brawl.

'That's so awesome, Louis. You don't have enough male friends outside work. I hope you plan to meet up again.'

He paused. He grabbed her empty wine bottle and set it on its side on the coffee table. It started to roll. 'There's a plan for that.'

'Excellent. Make sure you go.'

Just for a moment, he considered using her order as granted permission. But no. It would be deceptive, and she'd skin him alive for such trickery. He would have to come clean.

'Come sit here,' she said. 'Watch the end of this film with me. I'll fill you in.'

He'd literally opened his mouth in preparation for telling her everything. Now, the moment was lost. He sat by his wife. He'd wait until morning to tell the truth.

TEN

Louis had joined the Royal Navy in 1997, when he was seventeen. He was part of 3 Commando Brigade, - now renamed the United Kingdom Command Force - where he met Owen and Newton. The trio had been drawn together in part because they were all London boys. They served together in Iraq in 1999, in a non-combat role, but saw action in Afghanistan in 2002 as part of Operation Veritas. They had wild nights out and emotional huddles. They thought they'd be an inseparable team forever.

The first to shatter the bond was Newton, when he left in 2004 to spend more time with his lonely wife. Next, in 2006, was Owen, who was caught carrying cocaine by civilian police and dishonourably discharged. In 2008, Louis met Sonia at a library and knew he wanted her to be his world. He gave his one-year's notice and bowed out with a clean record and rank of sergeant. He and Sonia married the very next day.

The first couple of years of civilian life had been hard for Louis. In the army he'd witnessed deaths, even caused some, and the dark memories had had louder voices than the bright ones. For a long time he'd wondered if he had post-traumatic stress disorder.

A clinical assessment said otherwise and a psychiatrist offered another theory: Louis was institutionalised. He'd spent twenty-one of his twenty-two adult years in the Navy. It was all he knew. Back in the real world, he was a 'stranger in a strange land'.

This in mind, Louis got through the darkness by looking forward, not back. With separate lives, he, Owen and Newton had never found time to meet up following their service, although they'd kept in periodic touch by email and social media. He chose to cut all contact. His next step was to never talk about army life with Sonia or anyone who asked about it.

By the time his twins were born, in 2015, Louis was fully out of the tunnel. He hadn't contacted anyone from 3 Commando in years and hadn't spoken a word to anyone about his time as a soldier. Until Owen had appeared on his doorstep last night. After his old friend had left, Louis had wondered if it would be a bad idea to see his former colleagues. Would the subdued darkness take hold of his mind again?

It hadn't yet. In fact, the opposite had occurred. Now, as he lay under the quilt on this night, his thoughts turned again to his past, but did so with a sense of loss. He missed the brotherhood that the Navy had given him. His current social circle was pretty thin and he couldn't remember the last time he'd had a real belly laugh with someone other than Sonia.

He wasn't sure that he wanted to join Owen's operation, but he certainly wanted to stay in touch with his boys. Newton for sure. He could meet Sonia finally. They could eat at his restaurant. But a rekindled friendship with Owen might bring risks. He had an air of trouble about him.

Or maybe they'd all drift apart again, especially if the silly

Saturday thing fell through. And maybe that would be for the best.

He was still undecided about his role in the operation when he woke that morning. While shaving, he spoke to his reflection.

'What's your plan, Louis? You think you'll end up shaving in a plastic mirror in a prison cell? You want to have some young thug use a razor like this to cut your throat?'

'Have you cut yourself?' Sonia yelled from the bedroom. She'd overheard a snippet.

'Just a flesh wound,' he called back.

He still wasn't sure about the 'operation' as he entered the kitchen for breakfast. Sonia had made him boiled eggs and toast. He sat across from her, ate one piece of yolky toast, and words fell out of him without warning. 'The lads want me to go out with them tonight.'

'That's good,' she said, smiling. 'Like I said, you need to see male friends more.'

Saturday was their weekly Netflix movie night. 'You don't mind if we cancel the film?'

'No, not at all. I can bring Loz round.'

Her best mate from down the road. So, he'd made a step forward by clearing his evening. That was a pretty big indicator that he was warming up to the idea of joining the lads on a foolish mission.

He took no second step, though. He could not go ahead with the plan without Sonia's approval, but couldn't bring himself to unload the truth. What was that an indicator of?

The chance was gone a few minutes later. Breakfast finished, she headed upstairs to change into her uniform. If he was going to tell her, it had to be now. Once she'd left for work, he might not see her again until clocking off time, and that was way past the deadline for giving Owen his answer. But how would he begin to tell such a mad story?

She came downstairs shortly afterwards, kissed his cheek, and headed for the door. He went with her. He urged himself to speak – another indicator?

Money. He could start by mentioning how much money was on offer. That would immediately interest her.

In the end, he said nothing beyond a goodbye. She got into a colleague's car. And vanished.

That was it, then. Game over. Nice knowing you, lads.

ELEVEN

Louis's kids had a Meta Quest 2, a virtual reality headset. It had a boxing game, which he loaded up. He fought three digital opponents before ripping off the device and dropping to his knees, sweating and panting.

Wow, he was unfit, at least compared to the Louis of twenty years ago. His punch timing and dodge reactions had seemed okay, though. However, he couldn't compare computer graphics to real-life opponents, who might have knives and accomplices. Now he felt stupid for trying to test his abilities via a game.

He showered and dressed for work, then headed out. Newton called as he was driving.

'You decided yet, wimp?'

'No,' Louis said. 'I need to clear it with my wife.'

'I wish I had a wife to clear things with. By "clear it", do you mean you're up for this?'

'I don't know. It's risky. We're old men, Newton.'

Newton laughed. 'Tell me about it. I just went to the gym to punch a speed bag. Wow, I'm still seeing black dots.'

A real gym? Louis decided to keep his virtual reality

assessment secret. 'I'm a bit worried about this thing. Gangs have knives these days.'

'And we'll have hardware, too. I just got a call from Owen. He's got outfits and weapons. Just blunt objects, though. That make you feel better or worse?'

'Worse. It could all go wrong and we could end up in prison. Why would you want to risk that?'

Newton was silent for at least five seconds. 'For me it's worth the risk. But I'm not sure it's a risk anyway. We're only scaring away some young fools. If I'm honest, though, I'm kind of looking forward to it. It'll be a cool buzz. I've spent too long teaching idiots a lesson with written warnings.'

'The pen is mightier than the sword.'

Newton laughed. 'We could write complaints about the gang. But let's get serious. You need the money, right?'

He did, badly. He'd trained in vehicle maintenance in the army, but his wife's car's had problems beyond what he could fix with simple tools, and they couldn't afford to take it to a garage. The kids were gutted that their gymnastics had been cancelled to save funds. The family had bills all over the place. He and Sonia worked part-time and the wages were nothing to write home about. 'I guess the cash wouldn't hurt.'

'You were always the sharpest one of the bunch,' Newton said. 'I need you on this.'

'I don't know, mate. I really don't.'

'If the money can sway you, then how about this: I'll give you my share. I'm not in it for cash. Three grand extra, Louis. An hour's work.'

Louis sighed. 'I don't know. I still need to see Sonia about it.'

There was a screeching sound from Newton's end. A horn honked. Newton swore.

'Will you live long enough with your driving?' Louis said.

'Funny man. That was the other moron's fault. Look, we

meet at eight tonight, so send me a text before the working day is done. One way or the other.'

Louis promised to make contact, then hung up. Now he had something meatier to chew over. Six thousand pounds, for an hour's work. That made things sweeter. And harder.

TWELVE

During his 11am rounds of Fields Shopping Centre, Louis got a message from Newton:

ASKED 'ER INDOORS YET?

He replied:

GOING TO DO IT NOW

...and set off to do so. He headed up the escalator and into Sunny Zone, where his wife's store was located. He wasn't yet sure what he would say to her, but an event decided things. A pair of kids about thirteen years of age were running down the up-escalator, pushing past shoppers. Louis stepped into their path.

'Back up,' he told them.

'Piss off, dick,' one said. 'Get out of the way.'

'Back up or I'll bar you and the horse you rode in on.'

The kids objected no further and turned around. They raced to the top, again barging aside people minding their own business. When Louis got to the upper floor and stepped off, he heard a voice shout, 'Oi, security pussy.'

Off to the left and striding towards him was a man in his twenties with tattoos on the backs of his hands and his neck. He wore ripped jeans and a baggy T-shirt. He got real close. 'You call my brother a wanker, did you?'

Behind the goon, the two kids were watching and laughing. Tattoos didn't like Louis's pause and grabbed his elbow. 'You listening, twat? Who do you think you are to boss kids around?'

'Shift your grimy fingers. That's assault.'

The hand remained. 'You want me to show you assault? What kind of pussy picks on kids?'

'The hand. Last chance.'

The guy squeezed harder. Louis slapped the man's hand, hard. Annoyed, the guy hawked up phlegm and fired it right into Louis's face.

Before he could think of a response, Louis made one. He grabbed the guy's right arm with his, raised it high, and thundered a left fist into the exposed armpit. The blow agitated a whole bunch of nerves and gave Louis time to grab the goon in a neck-lock. A simple bulldog choke this time.

'Time to leave, friend.'

The guy struggled, but he had to follow his own head and Louis had it tight. He walked nice and quick to the exit. It was quite a sight for the shoppers, some of whom applauded. The kids followed, one bellowing for his brother to fuck Louis up. But the goon realised he faced a better foe and, when released outside, opted only for a verbal and profane response.

'You're barred until 2050,' Louis said as he walked inside. He watched the entrance from a distance, but none of the trio returned.

Unlike Newton, Louis wasn't game for action, but his muscles buzzed with adrenaline and the feeling wasn't uncomfortable. It had felt good putting that troublemaker in his place and making the shopping centre more peaceful because of it. If residents of an estate were so terrorised by thugs that they'd pooled money to buy help, then help they'd damn well get.

If his wife cleared it, of course.

THIRTEEN

Sonia was serving a customer when Louis stopped by the large front window of her store and waved. The customer caught her return wave and looked, and also waved. The women laughed about something as the sale was completed.

Sonia got a free moment shortly afterwards and exited the store. She and Louis stood at the balcony and stared down at the throng of shoppers moving about on the ground floor.

'Don't you just get the urge to start lobbing water balloons down?' she said.

'Sure, and that's why I don't carry them.'

'I think about some of their lives sometimes. I wonder how many have lost partners. How many are facing money problems. How many are badly ill.'

'I wonder how many are shoplifting.'

'Right. Hey, remember No Secrets Hour?'

Sure he did, for he had invented the game half a year into their relationship. Once a month, each person would be allowed one hour to snoop in the other's house. They would have free rein to search drawers, read mail, examine mobile phones or diaries. It had been amusing, even though Sonia had said that it felt like an exhibition of mistrust.

After they'd moved into their own flat together, the game had transformed into a verbal one. A partner could ask any question they liked, which had to be answered truthfully. Now content with each other and fully trustful, they hadn't played the game for years. But apparently Sonia wanted to right now.

'You think I'm hiding something?' Louis said.

'You know what you've never won? An Oscar. Because you're no actor. I know you're hiding something. You've been acting off, though. Ever since last night. Since you saw your old team.'

'So ask questions.'

'No. I'll just jump to the part where I say, "Pack your bags and enjoy your new whore".'

He scanned her face. Sonia wasn't one for wisecracks, but she had her moments and they were sometimes hard to discern. He quickly decided she was kidding. She didn't suspect he had another woman. But she knew something was up.

So he told her. Just like that. Three sentences, nineteen words, over in seconds. He waited for her response the way a blindfolded man might wait for a gallows trapdoor to open.

She gave him a look that said she, too, was reading his face for a jest. And then a glare that said she knew he was serious. 'So you boys got together?'

She was leading up to something he wouldn't like. He had to play along. 'Yes.'

'You had a drink, a little chat, reminisced about old times?'

'Yes.'

'And then decided it would be nice if you could all become superheroes again.'

'It's not like that. Owen picked guys he thought he could trust.'

'The old killing team back together for one last job?'

Oh, she was deeply annoyed. He wished he'd kept his mouth shut. 'He thought we could help out some people. It's six-and-a-half grand, Sonia. Enough for us to fix the car up. Pay for a long-awaited holiday somewhere. That can ease some worries.'

'And create a new one. Like my children's father getting himself stabbed in the heart by a crackhead. At least three grand will be enough for the funeral.'

He let out a laugh before he could stop it. He might as well have spat at her. 'You're laughing at me? Laughing at your silly, paranoid wife?'

'There's no funeral, Sonia. These idiots will run at the sight of grown men.'

'Men who should know better than to mess with the wrong people.'

Now he was annoyed. 'I faced real danger when I was in the army, Sonia. That didn't seem to worry you. You used to like telling your friends that I was out fighting for Queen and country. You loved having the big commando boyfriend. How many times did you insist on sex while I was in uniform?'

They seemed to be playing a new game involving one-upping the other's frustration. She won. 'You moron. I worried every day you were out there. But that was your job. You'd been trained. You were young. You were eager. Now you're–'

'What, out to pasture and lazy? It's not a gunfight, babe. It's some young fools who need the kind of slapping their parents never gave them.'

She nodded, but it wasn't in agreement. 'Yes. That's a very good term. Out to pasture. That's you. Has been for years. So please screw your head on right and wise up.'

His anger deflated in an atomic second. He couldn't counter

her argument, could he? His army days were long behind him. So were good knees.

'Wait a minute,' she said. 'Are you talking about tonight? Is that why you said you wanted to meet your friends again? Did you lie so you could go crack some heads?'

He'd been rumbled. 'I didn't lie. That would involve telling you we were doing something else. Never did that.'

'And would you have gone and not told me afterwards?'

Would you have gone – that sure didn't bode well for a future line like *Have a good time, sweetie.* 'Actually, no. The truth is I promised to ask you first.'

This was a curveball. She gave a thoughtful silence before her response 'So ask.'

'What do you mean?'

'Ask me.'

She'd thrown a curveball of her own. He babbled the words, 'Can I go?'

If that made him feel like a child, she got it and ran with it. She gave him a line to repeat. He jokingly told her piss off, but she insisted. If he wanted her permission, he had to word his question the way she wanted.

Shaking his head, Louis said, 'Please may I go out with my macho friends tonight because we're all having a mid-life crisis and need to prove that we can hang with the big boys?'

Annoying timing sent a pair of young girls past at that very moment and they giggled. Sonia said, 'How are you supposed to tell them your answer?'

'By text to Newton.'

She demanded his phone and, very reluctantly, he handed it over. As she worked with his device, she said, 'Get hurt and I won't forgive you.'

'I won't.'

'Get arrested and I'll dump you.'

'Deal. Custody of one kid each?'

She was not amused. She handed his phone back. He had a funny feeling about what she'd done and checked his messages. Sure enough, she'd sent one to Newton.

> THIS IS 'ER INDOORS. LOUIS CAN GO ON
> YOUR LITTLE PISSING CONTEST. I'LL
> HAMMER ALL OF YOU IF HE GETS HURT.

Shit. She'd read the message in which Newton had called her a derogatory term. As soon as she knew Louis had read her reply, she turned and, without another word, headed back into her store.

'We need a tough attitude like that,' he called after her. 'Maybe you should come along and help.'

No response. But there was one from Newton, and it sounded as if he thought Louis might have pretended to be his own wife:

> GOOD BOY. DON'T WORRY, WE'LL BE MORE
> THAN A MATCH FOR A LITTLE GANG.

He was more worried about his wife's wrath than that of a bunch of thugs.

FOURTEEN

On Saturday morning, Owen rode his pushbike to Parry Estate, which was peaceful at the moment. It sure wouldn't last. He headed down an alleyway between two end terraces and flew by a pair of residents talking over their backyard fences. He ducked his head as if he might interrupt their chat by momentarily breaking line of sight to each other.

The house he wanted was across the road at the end of the alleyway. He blew out into the open without a care for traffic, and a Mondeo nearly wiped him off the earth. The driver looked horrified, and again when Owen gave her the finger.

He went round the back of the house and heaved his bike over the high fence, then climbed after it. He knocked and soon after a face pressed against the frosted glass, trying to discern who her visitor was. Owen was the only person to use the back door, but she never seemed to remember that.

'This is a burglary,' he said. 'I forgot my crowbar.'

The door opened and a woman in her early sixties stared at him with scorn. The perfume necklace was around her neck again and she already stank of the stuff. 'Same old joke, Owen. Same old disapproving face, you notice?'

'I tweak the words a bit each time. And I only do it because you always give me that look up against the glass when I come.'

She eyed him up and down. 'Same old street brute outfit again.'

He liked tracksuits – so what? 'Ever thought how daft I'd look riding my bike in a suit?'

'A suit would look fine in a car,' she said, and turned away, heading into the house. Owen followed, sighing. The car shit again? Well, he wasn't going to feel guilty about having made nothing of his life. Parents made their kids, he believed. And what could anyone do with a mother as fucked up as his?

The living room was ordered mess, as usual. The ornaments on the mantelpiece were spaced exactly the same distance apart. The two sofas were perfectly parallel to the walls with a five-inch gap. Yet her dolls, which she made and painted and sold online, were scattered everywhere, in various stages of construction or deconstruction – or dismemberment, as Owen thought of it.

The room was a paedophile's charnel house. Owen had to move a set of hips and legs to find a spot on a sofa. The toes of the doll's legs had painted nails, which made him feel nauseous.

She brought him water in a beer mug commemorating the marriage of Prince Charles and Lady Diana, which was the only drinking vessel she had. Then she stood in the middle of the room and sprayed herself with perfume. He bet it was at least the tenth time that morning.

'So what do you want, Owen?'

'I came through. You people wanted help with the scum round here, and I got it. I got guys willing to scare these little nobs away.'

'Left it to the last minute, didn't you?'

Always scathing, this bitch. Never a word of praise or thanks. Then again, he knew he was silly to ever expect her to change. *A son is meant to be a good investment*, she had told him more than once. She was always moaning about all she'd done for him. All that effort expended in changing his nappies, buying him toys and food, using petrol to pick him up from school. Now he was supposed to repay all that shit. She treated him like a goddamn pension.

He'd hit back once: 'Fuck you, Mum. If you wanted to make money out of me, you should have sent me to film school or bought me a fucking tennis racket when I was a baby.'

He was saved from today's lecture by the doorbell. She got up to answer it. Owen sat there and looked around the room. His own place was cheap and tacky, but this was another level. Not long after Owen had been booted from the Navy, his father had died, and it had cracked her mind. There was probably a long medical term for what she had and whole books explaining it, but Owen liked to keep things simple: she was fucked in the head.

His train of thought derailed as he heard raised voices from the front door. His mother was trying to convince someone that Owen wasn't here. But the owner of the other voice was a guy he knew would never accept someone's word. Owen got up and rushed to the door.

On the step were three guys. Sam, his drug dealer, wearing the same coat and same beanie hat from yesterday. With him were a menacing pair of brutes.

Last time, he'd been subdued by Sam's presence at Sally's front door. But this was his mum's house and that made him angry. 'What the hell are you doing here?'

Sam looked awed. It was rare that someone gave the gang leader such attitude. The brutes made no move, but Sam put his hands out to block them. It seemed like a pantomime. 'Steady on, boys. Who the fuck do you think you're talking to, Moore? I'll gut you. Say that shit again if you dare.'

Owen got his anger under control. The last thing he needed was a melee on his ma's doorstep. She'd only hold it against him. He pulled and pushed his mother and got her through the living room door. 'I'm sorry, man. I was already worked up. I didn't mean anything.'

'Give me attitude again, Moore, and your fucking mum there will need a black dress. You piece of shit. You want to know why I'm here? For you. To make sure you remember what you owe.'

'I do. A grand on Sunday night. I'll be getting the money, I promise. And you'll be getting what you're owed.'

Sam nodded. He removed his beanie cap for a moment to scratch his head. Owen found it amusing that Sam hated his ginger hair but loved his nickname of Ginger Ninja.

Owen smiled, and said, 'You've been owed it for a long time, Sam. And you'll get what's coming.'

That was a risky line, but Sam missed the threat. He wouldn't miss the carpet bombing he and his cronies had coming tonight.

FIFTEEN

At the end of Carter Road – the only vehicular access into Parry Estate – was a roundabout with a superstore on the far side. The boys parked here in preparation for their meeting, but staggered their arrivals.

First to arrive was Newton, at 8.15pm. He followed Owen's instructions to use a small field alongside Carter Road, so as to remain unseen. Newton parked in a lay-by on the main road and climbed over a low wooden fence. The sky had been dark for almost an hour.

As he jumped off the fence, into the empty field, he heard a noise to his left and jumped. His own noise made the guy lurking in the trees look his way. He was a weedy kid of about twenty, taking a piss against a trunk. He quickly tucked himself away and vanished.

Carter Road ran alongside the eastern edge of the estate and curved to enter it from the north. It was here, on the bend, that he found Owen hiding behind the lip of a grass berm erected by RAF Northolt to suppress airbase noise. Owen was watching Parry Estate through binoculars. A large rucksack lay beside him.

'Jesus, Owen. Overkill.'

Owen snorted. 'Get down. The gang will be on the green soon. And there's the spotter.'

'What do you mean?' He could see the green that Owen referred to: a half-circle of grass inside the curve of the road. And he could see the spotter down near the end of the road, about 200 metres away. He sat in a bus shelter and played on his phone. His job was to report unknown visitors, hence why Newton had used the field.

'How do you know they'll come to the green?'

'It's their Saturday thing. I'll tell all when Louis gets here.'

'What's in the bags? The outfits? I pray it's not Navy uniforms. That would be so cheesy.'

'Wait and see.'

At 8.30, Louis parked in a superstore across the main road from the field. He crossed that road and clambered over the fence, to virtually mirror Newton's journey. When he found his friends, he got behind the berm and pointed at the bags. 'The outfits you mentioned? Better not be dressing us up as something silly, like pirates or superheroes.'

'You'll see,' Owen said. 'Hands off till it's time.'

Louis turned away from the estate, to stare across the fields, at the lights of the airbase. Newton noticed. 'Jealous?'

'No.'

'RAF weeds?' Owen said with scorn. 'You see any need for planes here? Us Navy boys can handle this.'

'I don't see any boats, either,' Newton said.

Louis was in no mood for banter. 'Okay, we're here. Let's hear the plan, Owen. And see what's in your goodie bag.'

SIXTEEN

The Ninja Warriors wasn't the only gang in town. There were myriad groups of likeminded youngsters across the city. Each had its home patch and by unwritten rule outsiders didn't invade another's domain. But they all sought control over unclaimed areas – what Owen referred to as 'high seas'.

The term got a laugh from Newton. 'You make these gangs sound like major organised crime groups.'

'No, no. I'm not talking about control of towns. I mean things like areas outside shops and playparks and stuff.'

Newton laughed again. 'Playparks? Like slides and roundabouts and things? Are these gangs of toddlers?'

'Be serious, dude. I just mean sometimes little thugs like to hang around places, and they don't want to be messed with by other gangs. Yeah, like playparks. Street corners. And we've all seen how kids like to doss outside shops at night.'

'In the light. Like moths. Anyway, what's your point.'

'I was getting to that if you hadn't interrupted,' Owen said. 'There's a gang called E55. Twats named after some bus that goes down their street. It's a mile from here and in between there's a waste ground the council recently cleaned up and paved over. It's empty at the minute. Good spot for motorbike racing and basketball. E55 want it and The Ninja Warriors want it. Tonight they fight for it.'

Louis said, 'Fight? I hope you're not talking about some Braveheart-style battle.'

'No. Right there on the green. A boxing match. One versus one. E55 are sending a guy. The rule is no other outsiders are allowed on this patch. All the Warriors will be there.'

'What's to stop them attacking the one guy?'

'Rules. Honour. Pride. Laugh if you want. I reckon that's pretty professional. So, we're talking about maybe fifteen Warriors.'

His friends didn't like this number and Newton let it be known. 'That's a lot, Owen. We can't take fifteen.'

'No, we take the leader. The king. Like chess. It's over when the king goes down.'

Louis wished he'd stayed at home. But it was too late to back out. He asked if they could see the outfits. And sorely regretted it seconds later.

'What the hell is this?' Newton said, holding up a white one-piece costume with built-in hood and mask. They had walked further down the backside of the berm, so they could stand up and be hidden from eyes in Parry Estate.

Owen tossed Louis a red costume and took the black outfit for himself. 'Ninjas. Real ninjas.'

Louis wanted the ground to swallow him up. 'I would have preferred the pirates,' he said. If he thought things couldn't descend further into the comical, he got a reality check when Owen produced weapons. Wooden samurai swords with black tape around the grips and blades painted silver.

'Katanas. Check these bad boys out.'

Newton held his sword as if it was made of dogshit. 'This is a joke, right? A wind-up.'

Owen wasn't laughing. 'Not to the Warriors. Just imagine their faces when three ninjas come running down the hill, waving these things. Ninjas scared the shit out of me as a kid.'

Ninjas had scared Louis as a kid, too. But back in the 80s, when they featured in a host of cheesy action flicks. He found them pretty laughable now and reckoned even today's children did. 'Thank God the gang isn't called the Barbie Boys.'

His joke seemed to ease a little tension. The boys dragged their outfits on. Newton had a pot belly and it was a struggle. When he finally managed it, everyone laughed.

'You look shrink-wrapped,' Louis said.

'Jesus, I can't wear this.'

'Hey, I went to a lot of trouble here.' Owen said. 'Hoods and masks.'

'No pissing way,' Louis said.

'Then let everyone see your face.'

Louis bit back his shame and pulled the hood over his head. Newton copied, then posed with his sword. The three old friends stood in a circle and insulted each other. Newton's black face stood out against his white gear. Owen's beard made his head wider at the bottom than the top. Louis's junk was clearly visible.

'At least we're having a laugh before we get slaughtered,' he said.

'At least this can't get any worse,' Newton offered.

'Spoke too soon.' Owen dipped into the rucksack and produced a plastic bag full of what looked like eggs painted black. 'Smoke bombs.'

'Jesus Christ.' Newton turned the tip of his sword blade to his chest. 'Anyone else for seppuku?'

SEVENTEEN

At 9.30pm, it all started to happen, and quick. Three young men walked onto the green, one carrying a satchel and another bearing four traffic cones. These were set up in a square to create a boxing ring, with tape strung between them.

'They're just going to do this right out in the open?' Newton said.

Owen nodded. 'Every Saturday. Nobody says shit about it. At least they're not hassling the residents.'

Three more guys sauntered over from the estate. Two cars came, each ferrying a pair of young men. Two more Warriors arrived on pushbikes, one a girl, and another on an offroad motorbike.

'That's The Ginger Ninja,' Owen said upon the appearance of another man, who walked over from behind the shop at the end of the main road. 'He lives above that shop.'

This puzzled Louis. 'I don't get it. Some of these bozos live here? Why don't people get them evicted? And what about parents?'

'This ain't a quaint village. Not everyone is friends. The

Ginger Ninja lives alone. Two others live alone. There's only one who lives here with his mum and dad, and they're slimeballs as well. Like I said, nobody wants to get a bullseye on their face.'

They watched for another few minutes. No others came. In total there were fourteen enemies on the green. Which became fifteen when a guy on an electric bike rode up Carter Road.

'That's the E55 guy,' Owen said.

Louis grabbed the binoculars. The cyclist had a pair of boxing gloves dangling from his handlebars. He watched the kid ride past the bus shelter. Sitting inside it, the spotter made a call on his mobile. Louis panned to The Ginger Ninja, who took that call and yelled to his people that it was 'game on'.

When the new arrival got to the green, he dumped his bike and stepped into the ring. He punched into his gloves and began shadow boxing. All the warriors lurked by the other side, keeping their distance, and nobody said a word to their enemy. Louis had to admire this kid's gallantry for travelling alone to fight in hostile territory.

One of the Ninja warriors wore shorts and a T-shirt. He got boxing gloves from the bag that another had brought. The two combatants got into the ring.

'Will they just let E55 guy go if he wins?' Newton asked.

'Dunno. I've seen four of these fights and the Warrior guy has never lost.'

The boy in question got his gloves on and stepped into the ring. He was short, but well-built. The two combatants started eying each other up. Insults were thrown.

Owen picked up his wooden katana. 'Get ready, boys. By the way, nobody touch The Ginger Ninja. He's mine.'

Newton said, 'Can't we watch the boxing first?'

Apparently not. Owen leaped out from behind the berm,

raised his sword high, and let out a roar. Everyone across the way looked. Owen started running down the hill. The sight of it clearly dispelled any shame Newton felt about this whole set-up, for he, too, bolted down the hill. Louis sighed and was soon hot on their tail.

EIGHTEEN

'Ninjas!' one of the Warriors yelled. She pointed. Heads turned. Mouths dropped.

The Warriors might have stood their ground against even double the number of enemies thundering down the hill. But what they saw was surreal, alien, and that made the difference. The fight-or-flight response took control. There was no fight. The mass of young men and women blew apart as if a bomb had gone off in its centre. They fled in all directions.

Newton aimed at one of the cars. Just as four thugs hopped in to make their escape, he leaped onto the bonnet and drove a heavy foot into the windscreen. His boot went straight through. He yanked it out, dropped to his knees, and stuck his sword inside, pointed at the driver's throat.

In a comically fake Japanese accent, he yelled, 'I see you around here again, I come kill. Understand?'

All four guys in the car nodded. Newton leaped off the bonnet and scanned for another victim.

He chose the guy who had the dirt bike. The kid, who looked only about eighteen, kicked it into life land eaped away. He saw the white ninja coming dead ahead pulled a wheelie, to put thick metal and rubber between him and danger. Newton sidestepped and brought his sword down on one of the biker's arms, which ripped his fist from the handlebars.

When the bike's front wheel hit the grass, the rider was unable to control the thump with a single arm. The bike fell and the rider tumbled across the field.

Newton was on him a second later: a foot on the neck, a sword-point against the cheek. He didn't bother with a silly accent. 'The next time you idiots cause any trouble in this estate, we'll be back to make you seriously regret it. Understand?'

The kid nodded.

'You got a job, boy?'

'College,' the kid moaned.

'Stick to that.' Newton released him. He got ready for an attack, but the biker hustled to his machine and abandoned the area. Newton's gaze fell on another Warrior and he gave chase.

Louis chose the weakest kid of the bunch, who just happened to be the one the Warriors had chosen to fight for them. Ditched by his gang, he'd remained in the ring, frozen in fear. Louis leaped the tape and walked towards him, sword-point leading the way.

'Don't hurt me, man,' the teenager moaned. He held his gloved hands up. 'I din't do anything.'

Louis touched the boy's T-shirt with his sword. 'We have eyes and ears everywhere. If you come back here, you'll wish you hadn't.'

'I live here.'

'Then make sure you keep out of trouble. Stay indoors after dark. Don't be hanging around with these idiots. Read books. Learn French. Help old ladies across the road. Right?'

'Right. Sure. I promise.'

'Now get lost.'

The kid got lost. He was the last to do so. The land was clear of Warriors. Louis saw Newton approaching. The restaurant owner whooped with glee and Louis smiled beneath his mask. They high-fived each other.

'That was bizarre, but utterly awesome,' Newton said.

'Gotta admit, I didn't hate that as much as I thought I would.' He looked around. 'Where's Owen?'

They cast their eyes about. Owen was nowhere to be seen. Nor was The Ginger Ninja, the man he'd targeted.

NINETEEN

Around the back of the corner shop on Main Street was the walled yard where a shed containing gas bottles had been torched just days earlier. The flat above the shop was rented by The Ginger Ninja, and it was his safe space. So, when he saw three blokes dressed as damn ninjas come bombing his way, home was where he fled.

The yard was accessed down a short, dead-end side street. The gate into the yard was missing and instead Sam had placed a mesh roll cage stolen from the nearby supermarket. Moving it slowed him down and Owen was upon him before he'd created a big enough gap to squeeze through. Hearing his enemy's approach, Sam turned, and caught a wooden sword right across the nose. His legs gave out. As he fell, his beanie hat slipped off his head.

'Let's go have a chat,' Owen said. He kicked the cage aside, grabbed a handful of ginger hair, and dragged his prey into the littered yard. He dumped him on his back. 'Why you got so much hair if you hate the colour?'

Clutching his leaking nose and kicking his heels against the battered concrete because of the pain, Sam yelled, 'You're fucking dead for this. I'll find out who you are. I'll fucking make it my life's mission and–'

He stopped as, in that moment, he fulfilled his life's mission. Owen yanked down his hood to show his face.

'Moore. You're fucking dead for this. You and your bitch freak mum. I'll fuck her up with–'

Owen stamped on the hands closed over Sam's face, which further broke his nose. Sam screamed in pain. The upper back windows of a row of houses on a nearby street were visible over the wall, but there was no angle for anyone to see the ground. Owen squatted to be out of sight. He extracted a knife from his sock. He put the blade under Sam's chin, which acted like a kill switch for all his panic and pain. Sam froze and stared up at him.

'You didn't ask why,' Owen said. 'Go on.'

Sam didn't ask why at first: he machine-gunned more insults and threats. But he relented after a jab from the knife into his neck. 'Why then? Fucking why, you piece of shit?'

'Sally. She's not your girl anymore. She's mine. I've watched you use and abuse my baby for months. That shit's all over now. Isn't it?'

It would seem not. Calmer now, Sam said, 'I'm going to have her raped, Moore. By ten guys a day, every day. All because of you.'

Owen smiled. 'Would it help if I said sorry and walked away?'

'You better run to the moon, arsehole. You just made the biggest mistake in history.'

'No, ginger twat, you did that. The day you first laid a hand on Sally. You're never going to hurt her again. Or anyone else. Have a good, long think about why I just took my mask off.'

Owen smiled as he saw Sam's eyes widen with fear – and realisation.

TWENTY

Louis and Newton waited back at their berm hiding place for fifteen minutes, then someone spotted Owen coming along the dirt track. They'd already stripped off their ninja outfits and Owen had his balled in his hands.

'Where were you?' Louis asked when Owen was by their side.

Owen shrugged. 'Getting my guy. Good job, guys. They saw the error of their ways. There's one more thing.'

He stuffed the outfits into the rucksack and extracted a paper bag. He tipped out the contents. Three wads of cash, each tied up with an elastic band. He tossed one to each of his friends. Louis immediately flicked through it. £20 notes. Real ones. Right then he regretted nothing, but his shame factor increased.

'Maybe we could do this again,' Owen said. 'Once a week or month. Visit estates. Kick ass. I know you joked about it, but we could really be like the A-Team.'

'No way. One and done,' Louis said. But he wondered what his answer might be if Owen approached with a similar offer. The money felt good in his fingers.

Owen hauled his rucksack onto his shoulder. 'Shame I forgot to use the smoke bombs. Anyway, guys, that's me done for now. Got pressing business. I'd get going quick in case any of these guys come back heavy-handed. Or the cops come. I'll be in touch maybe.'

Owen saluted and started walking across the field, to wherever he'd locked up his bike. Newton and Louis looked at each other as if unsure what to do. Then they started walking.

At the edge of the field by the main road, they hopped the fence thirty seconds apart to avoid appearing as a memorable duo. Louis ran over the road to access the superstore car park and his vehicle. He waited for Newton, whose flash car drew into the bay next to his. They wound their windows down to chat.

'Keep in touch?' Newton said. 'It would be a shame if that was the end of it for another decade or more.'

Louis nodded. 'Sure thing. We can do snooker or dinner or a pub crawl. But no more of this silly shit.'

'You regret it?'

The cash was very nice. But was it the major factor? He had to admit he'd enjoyed the action a little. 'A little. I kind of wish we hadn't done it. Not sure I would have without payment.'

Newton lobbed something through the window. It was the wad of cash from Owen. 'My share, as promised. And there's more where that came from. Anytime you decide the part-time security guard life isn't for you, let me know. I own a restaurant.'

'You offering me a busboy job?'

'No. I can have you trained as a manager. Good wage, good perks. Let me know. Have a good day, old mate. Hey, did this make you miss the old days?'

Louis shook his head, but thought for a moment and said, 'I miss them anyway, a little. Maybe. I don't know. You?'

'I've missed the old days for years,' Newton said, then buzzed up his window and drove away. Louis left the car park thirty seconds later.

When he got home, he parked and watched the front door, expecting Sonia to come running out. She didn't.

When he entered the house, he expected her to burst through the living room door. She didn't.

When he stepped into the living room, he expected her to jump up. She didn't.

She sat on the sofa, watching TV – but not watching at all. Because her hands were over her face, like a kid who can't bear a horror film. She said, 'Well, you drove home and walked in, so the damage can't be that bad. Are you scarred for life? I can't look.'

'Your husband is here and he's handsome.'

'So they did change your face, then?'

He laughed. She peeked through her hands, looking him up and down. He did a twirl to show he was fine and healthy. She ran to him. He thought she was eager to hug, but her hands felt his body for injuries.

'I'm fine, Sonia,' he said, laughing. 'It was no big deal, like I promised. We just gave some little thugs a scare.'

She stepped back. 'For the last time, I hope. You're not making a habit of this. I don't care about the money.'

'Are you sure?' He'd prepared for this moment. He'd put all the loose cash in a small bag, which he now raised above her head. He upended it to rain banknotes over her.

She didn't seem that impressed. 'No more, okay, Louis. Although this money is helpful, it's been earned immorally.'

'Okay, light up the fireplace. We'll burn it.'

'That was a wild and stupid one-off. Never again.'

He grabbed cash from the floor and stuffed it into her bra,

which finally got a big smile. 'No, seriously, I don't want a repeat of this. I don't want people getting injured, and I absolutely don't want to worry about you getting hurt.'

He pressed a banknote to her lips and kissed her through it. 'Worry ye not, baby. Nobody got hurt.'

PART 2

TWENTY-ONE

Although the yard out back of the shop in Parry Estate was the domain of the resident in the flat upstairs, the fifty-six-year-old shopkeeper used it for taking in deliveries. At 6am Sunday, while it was still dark, he entered his shop and unlocked and opened the back door, ready for the arrival of a van with soft drinks. End of plan.

He saw a shape lying by the back wall. A human shape. He wondered if it was a homeless man, but there was a large wet patch pooled around the shoulders. No homeless guy would sleep in a puddle. The man was dead. The puddle was blood. Bang went a day's trading. He called 999.

The BT operator patched him through to Metropolitan Police's Customer Contact Centre, where he told his tale. Soon the crime report made its way to the force's Homicide and Serious Crime Command, which passed it to the on-call murder investigation team, number six of eighteen.

Within that crew was another, the Homicide Assessment Team, a two-man set-up whose job was to head to a scene and determine if there truly a dead body and suspicious circumstances. Sometimes people died of natural causes.

Sometimes they weren't even dead. Only if the HAT guys hit the panic button did the rest of the team mobilise.

A detective called Sergeant Manning was part of the HAT, and by chance the lady on the rota with him was off that day. When he heard that the supposed dead guy was at the Parry Estate, he headed out alone. He parked down the dead-end side street and entered the rear yard. At that point the old, fat shopkeeper appeared at his back door.

'Go back inside,' said Manning. 'Shut those curtains so you can't see. Tell no one anything. Told anyone already?'

'No. They'd all come stomping down here for a look. I know that boy. I had a closer look. His name's Samuel Fritz. He lives in the flat above. He's a–'

'Fine, great,' Manning cut in. 'You got a car?'

'Yes. The Kia out front.'

'Go inside. Call no one and do nothing. And don't watch out the top window. Don't touch the flat upstairs.'

'You're gonna call blokes in, aren't you? Like, a whole squad. Will I be able to open the shop?'

'That'd be handy. My colleagues can take breaks to drink coke. The coroner can pop in for a sandwich. I hear he likes cheese and onion.'

'I've got that, and I've–'

Manning had expected his sarcasm to make the shopkeeper realise he was a dumbass. More fool him. He cut in with, 'You're not opening today. Do all those things I just said. But first, go put your keys in the ignition of your car. Don't ask why.'

When the shopkeeper was gone, Manning stepped closer to the body for his first real look. Blood everywhere and a big slash across the throat. The shopkeeper knew his stuff: this was Sam Fritz, dead at twenty-one. The way most expected him to go.

Manning got the shopkeeper's Kia and parked it across one lane of the side road. He used the HAT car to bar the other lane.

He didn't want to cordon off the area using crime scene tape because that would have been a shining beacon for the nosey. Few people would be awake this early and the longer he could keep this from prying eyes, the better.

Then he made a call.

The man who arrived half an hour later parked at the vehicle barrier and rushed to the yard. He was slightly overweight, tall, with a handsome face and brown hair surprisingly glossy for a man on the cusp of fifty. He wore a shirt, jeans, and a green suede jacket. Manning stood back and watched the man approach the body. The man squatted by the body and glared at it for well over a minute. Manning waited a respectable number of feet behind him.

'Who else knows?' the man said.

Manning cleared his throat. 'Just the shopkeeper. That's who found him. He's inside.'

'Go in there and make sure he's not on a conference call about it.'

While Manning did that, the man in the suede jacket pulled out his mobile. He called a woman and told her where he was. She immediately read the worry in his tone and panicked. 'Is it Sam? Is he okay?'

'Our boy's dead,' Ley Fritz told his wife.

TWENTY-TWO

Marie Fritz, a large woman ten years younger than her husband, arrived not long after the call. It was now around 7am and the estate was waking up. Sergeant Manning stood by the cars blocking the side street to make sure nobody got near the scene. Marie left her vehicle haphazardly in the middle of the main road and ran down the side street as fast as her large frame would allow.

When she burst into the yard, she immediately pushed Ley Fritz aside so she could see her son. He watched her kneel by the dead boy and cry and whisper. He tensed when her utterances became louder.

When she struggled to her feet whirled on Fritz, it was with a demonic face. He knew it well. 'This is all your fault, you bastard.'

Fritz wasn't instantly dismissive. From an early age, Sam had been obsessed with following in his daddy's footsteps, and Fritz had been unable to prevent it. When Fritz himself had sought no future other than rising to the top of a criminal empire, nothing had dissuaded him. He had seen the same determination in his boy, and hadn't done much to steer him onto another path.

Even worse, he had provided his son with help. He gave Sam a few whores to control, a small drugs line to manage, and a couple of local stores to provide protection for. His boy ran around like he was the bee's knees, but he had no real power or influence outside this estate.

Fritz had engineered that – what he called a 'demo' version of the lifestyle of a criminal kingpin. He likened it to a firefighter dad giving his kid a uniform and a hosepipe and a go-kart dressed like a fire engine.

Fritz hadn't seen a danger, but Marie had warned him that it was a bad idea to allow his son to play gangster, and look at the result. Their beloved Sam was dead in a grimy back yard. Fritz could hardly jump to his own defence now, could he?

So he said nothing and let Marie rant. He was a useless father, she said. He'd been unable to protect their boy, she moaned. He might as well have stabbed Sam himself, she wailed. He gave her a full minute to vent, then spoke.

'I was powerless to stop this, yes. But I can do something to make sure Sam's killer doesn't get away with it. I'll call Jim to–'

She grabbed a portion of a broken brick from the floor and lobbed it at him. Her bulk made bending and throwing slow, so he had plenty of time to prepare and dodge to one side. 'Jim? You think I'm about to let you get rid of my son's body? Are you insane?'

Jim had organised the disposal of many bodies, so Fritz understood why she jumped to such a conclusion. 'That's not what I meant, Marie. I know we can't pretend Sam's not dead. I just meant I want to get him out of here. I don't want him part of a crime scene. We want to control what happens, don't we?'

She seemed to mellow a little, but he knew why. She got a

matronly demeanour when she felt he needed schooling. 'I know your mind. You think you can solve this–'

'I will. I'll bring you the head of whoever did this.'

'Don't ever interrupt me. I know your brain. You plan to kill my boy's killer, hide all the evidence, then call in the police and let them run around like headless chickens. But we can't do that, Ley. We can't mess with a crime scene. You know the police are going to use this against you, right?'

He nodded. If someone got killed, family members were always going to be the first suspects. Even if they damn well knew Fritz didn't have his own boy whacked, they'd love an excuse to toss him in a cell for a day, grieving father or not.

She said, 'So, no hiding for you. We'll get that caper out of the way quickly, and then the police can properly get down to their investigation.'

'They'll do nothing, Marie. Look at who I am. Look at who Sam is. They'd rather solve a missing cat case.'

'I know that,' she said. Her face was still an angry mask, but her tone didn't match it. 'But you're a waste of space, remember? You killed my boy. A failure, that's you. You couldn't protect him like you swore to. So get the police, the professionals, and do it now. But I don't want them in my home, Ley. So go to one of your other places. Do you understand?'

He did. Marie stormed out of the yard. Fritz heard her car burst from the scene at speed. He almost wished he hadn't told her about Sam, at least while his body still lay in the crime scene. He wondered if the murder was going to tip her over a cliff edge she'd been precariously balanced upon for a while now.

He made a phone call on a fresh burner in his pocket. Instead of contacting Jim, he directly phoned one of the safe houses he operated. He picked the one in Greenford, which was closest to this area.

'Clean out the house for me. I'm coming over. So are the police.'

The man on the other line was probably bewildered, but he knew better than to seek enlightenment. Fritz hung up and yelled for Manning.

The detective came running. He found Fritz squatting by his boy again. 'Call it in as normal,' Fritz said. 'Start your homicide investigation. You heard a rumour that I was at 25 Penistone Road in Greenford. I'll be there and waiting. Make sure you keep me informed at all times about what your people are doing to investigate this.'

Manning nodded his understanding. 'Want me to try to be the interviewing detective? I might be able–'

'No. You stay on the periphery of this. I can't risk you being compromised. Just do what I said.'

'Sure, boss. Any clue who could have done this?'

As he walked away, Fritz said, 'Someone who right now has no clue he's a dead man walking into hell.'

TWENTY-THREE

For her five years' service at *Shapz*, Sonia was awarded a bottle of gin and flowers and fifty per cent off any item of clothing. That was two years ago and the flowers were long dead, the blouse had been ruined by bleach, but the alcohol had been saved in a cupboard for a special occasion. Owen's silly named Operation Kickass had been it, so she and Louis had emptied the bottle.

He wasn't good with spirits and had a raging headache and cotton mouth when she woke him on Sunday morning around ten. He spotted something wrong with her mouth. She had closed lips and looked like she was trying not to throw up.

'You okay?' he asked.

And then she did throw up, all over his chest. But the vomit was paper money. He sat up. 'Okay. Some kind of joke. Explain.'

'Last night I asked you how much of the cash I could spend on myself.'

He remembered that, although not much else. He'd told her she could spend whatever she could fit in her shut gob. 'Very funny.'

'A deal is a deal.'

She counted the money. £480.

'Always said you had a big mouth.'

'How about we go out and, while I'm spending this, we buy that new washing machine? And a new coffee table. We could look at weekend breaks.'

His head was still killing. 'How about you go and I lie here and die?'

She kissed his cheek. 'The kids need feeding. Don't forget that.'

'Not sure I can do that if I'm dead.'

By the time she'd left for work, he was still alive, so he got up to make breakfast for the twins. As he walked onto the upstairs landing, he heard Theo scream. He threw open the door. 'What's going on?'

Theo and Louise were sitting side-by-side on the floor, playing a game on their Xbox. Theo said, 'This zombie dog's killed me like four times.'

'Billions of kids have been on earth over the last two hundred thousand years. And you're the first one to ever say that line.'

Louise grinned at him. 'Has anyone ever said, 'The blue dinosaur-shaped house got eaten by the sun'?'

Laughing, Louis headed into the bathroom to pee. After, he looked at himself in the mirror. His thoughts turned to yesterday evening. Immediately after ninja-ing the gang of kids, he'd felt embarrassed. Later, while getting drunk, he'd felt like a criminal. Now it was a new day and he'd had time to reflect, so whatever his opinion this morning, that would probably be the shape of things forever. So, how did he feel now?

Good, actually.

TWENTY-FOUR

Owen hadn't expected Sally to have a punter before 8am, but as he raised his fist to knock on her door, he heard a male voice inside. Gutted, he slinked away and sat in a bus stop across the street, watching and waiting.

Fifteen minutes later, two young Asian men exited her bedsit, laughing and joking with each other. They got in a BMW at the kerb and drove away like happy little bastards. Owen tried to dampen his resentment by reminding himself she'd be out of this game soon. Hopefully, she'd had her last ever punter.

He went to her door and banged. When she answered, it was in a negligee. She looked surprised to see him. And happy to see the £20 note he flashed at her. She invited him in.

After sex, he dressed and extracted his wad of cash. 'Two and a half grand, like I promised. So you fancy going away?'

She was at the dressing table, fixing her lipstick, and looked round. Her eyes widened at the sight of the cash. 'Away?'

'A Sunday away with me. Let's go to the coast. We can stay the night, walk on the beach, play some fruit machines, have dinner. I was thinking Whitstable. You still got a car?'

She looked wary. 'Yeah, but I work. Are you going to pay for my time?'

He waved the cash again. 'I'll treat us. But I need to take care of some things first. Later today?'

'What I mean is, I charge by the half-hour, baby.' Unbelievably, she fished a calculator out of a drawer and did the maths. 'If we went now and stayed until this time tomorrow, that's twenty-four hours. I get it to 960, but I could do it for 800.'

A thirty minute romp here and there wasn't enough time or the right circumstances for her to see his true personality. If she went away with him, she'd learn how much he cared about her, and she'd get to know what a funny, kind man he was. £800. It was a lot of money, but well worth it if their day away convinced her he was someone she could settle down with.

Besides, if he spent a couple of hours on the rob up in Whitstable, maybe he could make half her payment back. A tourist spot like that would have many rich visitors he could work over.

She had her hand out for the cash. He said, 'Not yet, baby. Later.'

'I need money up front. If you go and I wait and you don't come back, I've wasted time when I could have been earning.'

He loved her, but he didn't trust her one jot. Instead, he pulled a ring off his middle finger. He'd been planning to pawn it. It was a silver signet with a Chinese symbol engraved on the face. Her eyes lit up. 'Nice. But what's it worth?'

'A grand,' he said, with no idea if that was true or not.

'What's the symbol mean?'

'Happiness. You take this now and give it me back for the cash later.'

Deal. She took the ring and slotted it into her bra. He said,

'Pack some stuff. Get the car ready. I need to go see to some business. How about later this evening?'

She smiled. 'Okay. Actually, it sounds good. Maybe I'll treat you to dinner and stuff. Certainly some of you-know-what. It's your time to do whatever you want, after all. If I go out now and hand some of this over to Sam, he won't be around today, so he won't know I'm gone.'

Owen grinned at her. 'Sam won't be around ever again, sweetie. He got killed last night.'

She literally dropped her lipstick. 'What?'

'Yep. I heard he got in a fight and got his throat slashed. So don't you worry about that guy ever again.'

She was frozen with her empty hand by her face, as if she thought she still held the lipstick. He leaned in and kissed her cheek, reminded her of their evening meet, then left with a happy stride.

TWENTY-FIVE

Ley Fritz ran various kinds of safe houses. Of his fifteen across London, ten were clean joints where his men could congregate and fugitives could hang out. Places like that were nondescript and wouldn't worry the cops, as long as the occupants were shifted in time. Three more houses were drug labs, but those could be sterilised quickly. One place was where his rapid response guys hung out, and again the property could be neutralised fast.

There was one other kind of safe house. 25 Penistone Road was it.

Just after leaving the scene of his son's murder, Fritz called Jim. To everybody in the organisation, Jim seemed to be the boss. He called the shots, but at Fritz's behest. Jim knew more about the workings of the firm than even Fritz himself and could probably do a better job of running it. He was also the only man on earth who could get away with calling Fritz a dumb dickhead.

Which he did when Fritz called him about his plan to use 25 Penistone Road as the scene of his arrest. The gangster turned off the history audiobook playing through his car's speakers. 'What's the problem?' he said.

'Did you forget what we do there?'

Fritz's heart sank: he *had* forgotten. 25 Penistone was the firm's sole romper room. And not the cosy kids play space variety. It was more the kind operated by paramilitary groups in Northern Ireland during the Troubles. A place for violent interrogation and lethal punishment. The cellar was awash in blood. There were bodies under the back lawn. Killing tools were everywhere. No way could that place be cleaned up before coppers kicked in the door.

Fritz put Jim on hold and quickly called Sergeant Manning, but it was too late. 'Sir, I already told my boss. He loves it and he's arranging the arrest squad right now.'

Fritz returned to Jim and told him. Jim needed only a second to think. 'Head them off. They'll still come to the house, but if they've already got you, they'll not be as eager. We'll have time to get everything out and burn the building down.'

Fritz ended the call. He knew what Jim had meant by 'head them off'. He called Manning back and got his location. Murder Investigation Team Six was based in Putney, so he drove right there, fast. He parked his car against the blue back gates, blocking them. He got out and sat on his bonnet.

In no time at all, two uniformed officers approached. They were probably beat cops, existing in a world of volume crime, and they didn't recognise him. They called him sir and asked what he wanted.

'I'm saving the taxpayer petrol money. My son got murdered and you idiots will want to question me.'

The two cops looked at each other. One came right to the gate, to open it, and the other got his handcuffs out. Fritz said, 'Not you two. There's men in there who dream nightly of being the one to slap cuffs on me. They won't like their thunder being stolen. Call it in. Say Ley Fritz is outside.'

Handcuffs guy did that. When he got a response, the blood drained from his face. Fritz watched as, just half a minute later, what seemed like a whole platoon of officers burst from the building. They almost fought like kids to be the one to 'slap cuffs' on London's biggest, baddest, most untouchable crime kingpin.

TWENTY-SIX

The first time he ever got nicked, Fritz had been a simple hoodlum and he'd been booked in in the presence of his arresting officer and the custody sergeant. How times had changed. Two coppers held an arm each and another eight crowded the desk as the sergeant asked him if he knew why he'd been arrested.

'Same reason a castaway will suck seagull shit from a rock,' Fritz said. 'Desperation.'

Amongst the group were two men in suits with faces he recognised. High-ranking detectives who'd spent years being given the slip and now looked like kids at Christmas.

Fritz was polite and answered all questions. He kept his face impassive, although it wanted to settle into a default angry expression. These bastards knew his son was dead, but all they cared about was nicking a high-profile bad guy. He asked for a phone call, but one of the detectives said, 'Not yet, Mr Fritz. The phone is on the – ahem – fritz.'

The two detectives found that funny. Fritz had expected to have his allocated single phone call delayed. Too risky. They couldn't be sure, even if he called a priest, that he wouldn't utter a code word that would impel an armed rescue team down to the station. The whole building had probably been put on high alert. He imagined snipers on the roof and lowly police staff huddled under tables.

'Fair enough,' Fritz said.

But they had to go by the rules, so he was offered the duty solicitor. 'No, sir. The Legal Aid Agency sometimes takes ages to pay those chaps. I wouldn't want to deprive a man of his quest to own a Rolls Royce. That's what my own solicitor drives. But I don't need him today. Just get me to my cell because I didn't sleep at all last night.'

A man like Fritz in police hands and refusing a solicitor? He half-expected a cheer to go up.

The law gave the police twenty-four hours to keep him in custody, but it was standard to free someone after half that if they had no evidence and no reason to delay his release. Fat chance of that here, even though they damn well knew he didn't kill his own son. They'd hold him for as long as possible, just in case they could find something else to charge him for. To aid that, they'd delay his interview. Standard trickery.

However, he'd just told them he needed sleep. A fresh and rested man was sharper, and their best bet was to hammer someone with questions while he was below his best. Fritz knew a trick or two himself, and this one worked. Once he was locked in a cell, an officer kept opening the door every five minutes, making it impossible to sleep.

Fritz actually didn't mind the constant interruption. It kept his mind from sinking into dark depths. Within the hour he was called forth for a chat.

Burgle a house and the officers sitting across from you in interview would be a pair of detective constables. Not for Fritz. In the room was one of the detective inspectors who'd watched Fritz get booked in, and he'd been joined by a superintendent.

That meant there was a chance of Fritz getting an offer only a high-ranker could authorise. Perfect.

After the DI named all those present, for the recording equipment, Fritz looked at the super. 'Turn the tape off. I need the toilet.'

The super returned his glare, deep in analysis. 'We're not supposed to do that.'

Not, *We can't*. This guy hadn't taken the bait, but he'd seen it dangling. 'You know I didn't kill my son. This is retaliation, like all the traffic stops I get for not signalling. So there will be no charge. No court date. No one will review the recording of this interview. So no one outside this room will know you stopped the tape, which you're about to do right now.'

The super thought, and then told the tape he was pausing the interview so Mr Fritz could use the bathroom. But nobody moved afterwards. Fritz said, 'I walk out of here without charge, and you know it. You came in here with plans to hold me for the full twenty-four hours. I'm impatient. Release me now and I'll give you a bent copper.'

'What copper? What are you talking about?'

'Real release, of course. No pre-charge bail bull. Bail bull. I like that term.'

'What copper?'

'Not anyone associated with me. Just someone I know about. He's with the British Transport Police, B Division. He was part of Project Guardian about ten years ago. Ironic, that, because Guardian was all about tackling sex crimes on trains, and this copper...'

The super literally licked his lips. 'This copper...?'

'Raped a woman in a station when he was off-duty. But people knew, and now he pays a local gang to keep them silent about it. Won't matter to me one bit if that chap goes down.'

The super picked up his pen. Fritz slapped it aside. 'No

more info. You meet me outside at my car, and I'll give you the name.'

'Who killed your kid?'

'Write this number down. It's my solicitor. Get him here.'

The super bit his tongue. Fritz faked a loud laugh. The super then stood up.

Within half an hour, Fritz was escorted by two uniforms and the super to the back yard, where someone had parked his car. Fritz checked for damage, but there was none. He bet they'd been tempted to crash his ride, but were too worried he'd claim damages.

He was also certain the driver would have had a sneaky nosey around, but Fritz always kept his car clean just in case of a traffic stop search. His mobile phone was hidden in the engine compartment, untouched. When Fritz retrieved it, the super stared at the device like a dog spying a sausage.

He dismissed the uniforms. 'Okay. The bent cop?'

Fritz got in his car and buzzed the window down. He gave a name and said the rape occurred in November 2013.

'Thanks,' the super said, but he didn't sound grateful. 'Every other day, you're a vile criminal. But today also a victim. You regret bringing your boy into the fold?'

Fritz reached out to put his phone on the passenger seat. Nice and slow, so he could hide his face from the superintendent for a couple of seconds. The man had hit a nerve. When he faced the officer again, he started the engine.

'Who killed your kid?'

'Don't pretend to give a shit.'

'Don't confuse me with you. I work for justice and the law. There's a killer walking the streets, and he needs not to be. It doesn't matter about his victim or what the victim's father does for a living.'

'You'll never find my boy's killer.'

'I'll promise you right now, I'll do whatever I can to put this guy in prison. Just tell me what you know. Off the record, if needs be.'

Fritz realised the super had misunderstood. 'I wasn't saying you won't try. I mean he'll get justice and you'll never know about it.'

Now the super read between the lines. 'For once we want the same thing, Fritz. We shouldn't be in battle over this.'

Fritz started to buzz up his window. 'This isn't a battle. It's a race.'

TWENTY-SEVEN

Home was Kilton Park, on the border between Kent and Greater London. The exclusive gated neighbourhood boasted 140 residences across the same number of acres. It had woods, ponds, tennis courts, and a five-hole golf course. The cheapest properties cost more than a million pounds, while the upper end would set a buyer back fifteen times that.

Fritz's house was in the mid-range. It had four bedrooms, three bathrooms, a studio, cinema, and al fresco swimming pool. Fritz wasn't one for expensive champagne or flash cars or blinged watches, but his wife wanted a big house and he wanted somewhere safe.

And tranquil. He needed peace and quiet right now. The fact of his son's death was solid in his mind, but the effects of it were yet to strike. It could happen at any time and, when the bombardment came, he wanted to be somewhere comfortable and serene.

He entered the grounds through a security-guarded gate, and once parked outside his house, he sat thinking for a moment. Marie's car was here, but he didn't want to face her just yet, or the two bodyguards/butlers who lived in the property round-the-clock. He liked to listen to audiobooks and the one currently obsessing him was about famous shipwrecks. He put the volume only just loud enough to hear.

The expanse of trees all around made his driveway visible to only one other property, that of a Frenchman who'd invented a popular board game. Annoyingly, the man came out onto his lawn to mow, which disturbed the peace. Fritz shut down his car and headed to his house.

Marie had a few foibles that gave away her mood, and one was deep ambient music. He could hear it playing from the large kitchen as he entered the large vestibule. And it meant she was mellow, or attempting to get there. Even though he'd crept in quietly, one of his guards appeared in the doorway of the security room. Fritz knew he'd been clocked on the CCTV cameras. He waved the man away.

Marie was chopping potatoes, her back to him as she faced the wide window overlooking their large back garden. He sat at the kitchen table. 'I'm back.'

She didn't turn around. 'Released without bail? Did the police tell you if they know anything about Sam's murder yet?'

'Yes. And no. I still reckon they won't care.'

'And they won't be targeting this house?'

As part of an investigation into whether or not he'd killed his son? No. That didn't mean something else wasn't in the pipeline. 'You know that's always a risk, Marie.'

'I agree that the police won't care about our boy. So get off your arse and get hunting his killer.'

Earlier she'd warned him off investigating the murder. He was stunned by her change of attitude and made the mistake of saying so. Now she turned to him, wielding the potato peeler like a knife. But she looked calm.

'I was distraught, Ley. Now I've had time to think. What if my son's killer is someone like you? Highly-placed.

Untouchable by the police. What if they catch him and can't prove it, and he's released and put into witness protection? What if he's arrested and remanded, and a delay means he's not put on trial for years? What if he's given life but he doesn't mind prison? No, I want you to get out there and do it.'

He could direct any operation through Jim while right here with a phone at his ear, but knew that wouldn't go down well. She had meant it literally when she'd said she wanted him 'out there'. Any less and he'd be accused of nonchalance, of not caring about their son. He was too old for playing the all-action bad boy she'd fallen for all those years ago, but he really didn't want to fight with her.

He stood up. 'I'll go find this bastard right now. I'll torture the last breath out of him.'

'I'd like that very much,' she said with a smile, as if he'd suggested lunch on the back patio. She held out her arms. He moved into them. He'd long lost attraction towards his wife, but he liked being in her arms. There was something baby-like about how comforted he felt by a hug, although it was marred by the fact that they were blessing vicious, vengeful violence.

When she released him, she pointed into a corner of the worktop. There sat the vintage cast-iron receipts spike from his upstairs office. 'I want it there, baby.'

What? The spike? It was already there. He was puzzled. She saw it. 'What you promised me, Ley. Right there on the spike. His head.'

He felt cold as he looked for mirth in her eyes and saw none. She was deadly serious. He was London's top crime boss, feared no single man, and was responsible for many murders. But his insane wife sometimes terrified him.

TWENTY-EIGHT

For the first few years of his life, Ley's boy, Sam, had lived with his mother in Barnett. Fritz had visited often, but both parents had wanted to keep him a little distant for safety's sake. Fritz would often sneak away from his people to visit his son and take him to a children's playpark near the StoneX Stadium.

Often he went alone but on a few occasions, if it was late and teenagers hung around, he'd have one meaty bodyguard in attendance. Today, for his first visit in years, he took five.

They were there only to clean up. It was a Sunday afternoon and the park was busy with parents and kids. Fritz's heavies moved amongst them and one by one the parents dragged their kids away. The children were upset, obviously, but they'd perhaps be rewarded later with toys. Paid for out of the £200 Fritz paid each family.

When the park was empty, he sent four of his men on their way and stationed the last at the gate, to deflect new arrivals. Now alone in the park, Fritz lay back in the basket swing and pushed with his legs on the ground to get it moving. He stared up at the sky.

For years, every day, all day, he worried. It had never been any different. He couldn't remember more than a handful of times when he was at peace and not concerned about a vengeful thug in the shadows. That handful of times had occurred -

Voices. He looked over at the gate, where a mother and her son were talking to the thug manning it. The wiry-haired kid looked to be about eight, his skinny mother perhaps three times that and wearing a sling on one arm. The thug had a barring hand up and was shaking his head.

'Let them in,' Fritz called over. He couldn't take his eyes off the kid. He looked a little like Sam when he was that age. Same hair, same outward-pointing ears.

The thug stepped aside and the woman brought her kid in. The kid seemed to want to play on the basket swing, although his mother told him to find something else.

'No, he can have this,' Fritz said, getting off. The kid leaped on and the mother took a nearby bench. She thanked Fritz.

'Push me,' the kid called to his mother. For a few moments she did so, but one-handed wasn't able to get him arcing very high. The kid wanted Fritz to do it and the mother asked him.

Fritz was happy to. She sat on the bench again and Fritz propelled the kid nice and high.

That handful of times he'd felt free of worry? Right here pushing this swing, every time. Just like this. Him and his boy, alone, carefree, loving life. He felt the old stillness return. But he felt shame, too, because he was pushing someone else's kid.

And he couldn't forget that Sam was dead because his father hadn't kept him on a safe path. He should be out there, hunting the killer, just as he'd promised Sam's mother. But he needed this time to himself. The calm before the storm.

When the boy tired of the basket swing and scarpered elsewhere, Fritz sat on the bench.

'Your kid around here?' she asked.

'No. Elsewhere. I just came here to think. I'm sorry for my friend over there preventing you from coming in.'

'It's okay. We're here now. How old is your son or daughter?'

Fritz paused. 'I used to like bringing him here when he was about your boy's age. In fact, since he was about three. I miss it.'

'Oh, I know, they grow up so fast. There's a little park at the end of my street, but it's for fives and under. He's gutted. This one is for kids up to thirteen, but he'll be gutted again when he can't come.'

'They don't fancy it around that age anyway. They find other things. You have to keep an eye on them.'

'Don't I know it. My daughter, Lianne, she's fifteen and likes to hang out with friends at all hours. She's hard to control.'

'Don't let them get involved in crime. Always watch them. Don't let them hang out with the wrong crowd.'

'It's not easy. There's no father. But don't ask me about that.'

'Keep them on a leash or you'll regret it in the end.'

She was giving him a funny look.

He said, 'How did you bust your arm?'

She looked at her sling and seemed to be thinking about how much to tell him. 'Neighbour. He's bad news. He's got this new front wall and my boy muddied it with a football when we were having a kickabout on the street. My neighbour rushed out and tripped me to the ground. We should have been careful, I guess.'

'No, your neighbour should have.' He'd been here long enough. He stood. It was time for work. 'Anyway, have yourselves a nice day.'

'Good to meet you, sir.'

Fritz waved at the kid, who returned it, then he approached his man at the gate and said, 'Pay that woman the same money. And follow her home. She doesn't get on with the neighbour.

Make note of his nice new wall. Go back later in a heavy van that nobody can trace and make the wall no longer nice.'

'No probs, boss. And when the neighbour comes out moaning?'

'See that sling on her arm? I think he's jealous of it.'

TWENTY-NINE

At 12.30pm, Louis was in the garden shed, which he'd turned into a workshop. He was shortening three legs of the coffee table, an item he'd crafted right here and for years had been happy with. It was one of his original pieces, so he could overlook the error. That was how he convinced himself that he didn't also have to check newer items like the kitchen chairs, or the toilet seat, or the twins' toybox.

His mobile rang. It was Newton. He answered with a smile: he was off work today and fancied an afternoon out.

But his smile quickly faded. 'Someone died,' Newton said. 'That night, on that estate. One of those young louts.'

Louis thought he'd misheard. Someone was dead? They'd hardly laid a finger on anyone. Figuring the reception was bad in the shed, he exited and sat in the back yard on a stool he'd made from a log. 'What do you mean, someone's dead?'

'I mean that moron Owen killed someone.'

Louis' innards flipped. 'What the hell? No way. How do you know?'

'I just started my lunch break and checked the internet for anything about Parry Estate. And up it came. A man called Sam

Fritz got killed in the back yard of that corner shop. The Ginger Ninja. The man Owen was after. Go have a look and call me back.'

Louis' hands were shaking so bad he had to use voice search. He said, 'Parry Estate,' and got a list of web pages. The place was hardly a danger zone like Afghanistan or a gossip hub like Hollywood, so the murder story filled Google's first search page. It was right there in black and white, undeniable.

Twenty-one-year-old Sam Fritz, known locally as The Ginger Ninja, found dead in the back yard of his own property. Police called it foul play, although no post mortem had yet been performed. There were no other details about the death.

He called Newton, who immediately said. 'This is bad, Louis. That Fritz kid was the son of a crime boss.'

'Joint enterprise,' Louis said, his voice breaking between the two words. His hands continued to shake. 'We'll all go down for this.'

Newton was still on a different page. 'Never mind that, Louis. Son of a crime boss. Ley Fritz. I just looked him up. He's the most powerful gangster in London. He's got connections. This is real bad.'

Louis hardly heard him. 'We chose to go there. We had weapons. We set out to attack those gang kids. We'll get first degree murder for this.'

'Louis, listen to me. Forget the police. This Fritz man will be after us. We won't make it to a damn murder trial.'

Louis needed a moment to think. And he had to get out of the garden in case a neighbour heard the wrong thing. Newton was still talking, but Louis cut him off. He said he'd call back, then hung up.

He headed inside, upstairs, and sat on the toilet. He immediately dumped his bowels. He wondered if he should tell Sonia what had happened. There was a chance she'd disown him, but he couldn't let her discover the truth when the police booted the door in.

Now calmer, he turned his focus away from the police. Newton was more worried about the dead kid's dad, so he reloaded Google for a search of the term 'Fritz gangster'.

THIRTY

Leyland Ronald Fritz was born in November 1973 in Cyprus, where his father served in the 41st Marine Commando. A year later, when that unit was set to be withdrawn from the country, his mother relocated with her son back home to London. His father later died in a fight with another commando in his own barracks.

From an early age, Fritz knew how to make illegal money. By the age of ten, he was known to rent his services out to those seeking revenge. For a few pounds or even a bag of sweets, he would attack other kids, sometimes hospitalising them. By sixteen he'd fallen in with a notorious London gang and was employed as a burglar. He worked his way up to enforcer and beyond.

At the age of twenty-five, when the boss was jailed for murder and subsequently killed in prison, Fritz took over the firm. Some said Fritz framed the boss and ordered the hit.

Like any good crime lord, Fritz expanded his empire with legitimate businesses, in part to help hide illegal money from prostitution, drugs, smuggling, and a host of other shady endeavours. He started to rub elbows with kosher businessmen and even some celebrities, much as the Kray Twins did in the 1960s.

Suspected of ordering more than a dozen murders, he was a top police target and had been arrested many times. He'd won nine trials for a plethora of crimes. Not once had he been jailed and, these days, Ley Fritz was too powerful to even charge, never mind convict.

His fame and wealth made him and those closest to him a target, so in the late 1990s he sent his mother to live back in Cyprus and gave up contact with a scattering of relatives. Someone got to her anyway and she was killed in her home by a supposed burglar. He vowed never to have kids, but that changed when he met a barmaid called Marie at one of his legit nightclubs in Barnet. Sam Fritz was born eighteen months later.

After reading this biography, which glossed over Fritz's crimes and reeked of a journalist worried about comebacks, Louis called Newton. He was now far more concerned about Fritz than about the police. They had rules to follow. Fritz didn't.

'We need to talk to Owen,' Louis said. 'I know he said he wanted The Ginger Ninja, but we need to know for sure he did it. It's possible some enemy of Fritz's got to his boy.'

'I agree,' Newton said. 'I got a postcode for Owen. We'll go see him. I don't want to do this on the phone. But don't get your hopes up. This is on us, and that dead kid's dad for sure will send a platoon of goons out looking for us.'

THIRTY-ONE

Rather than 'platoon of goons', Ley Fritz used the term 'knuckles'. As he drove away from the playpark, he phoned Jim and told him to get knuckles on the street. 'Get me some leads. Someone always knows something. Get answers before the police do.'

He knew nothing yet, which grated on him. The last he knew, his boy had been at home in his dowdy flat. Fritz had offered to buy Sam a decent house in a nice zone, but he was his father's son and luxuries didn't interest him. He wanted to live on the shitty estate where his crew hung around.

His crew? A bunch of idiots who thought they were mobsters. They were chicken hearts who'd wilt when real hard cases turned up to ask questions. Fritz figured he'd know more about his son's killing within a couple of hours.

That would give him time to visit Floating Point.

He put the burner phone aside and grabbed his main device. He had many voicemails and texts. On the criminal side of his world, nobody would dare ring the boss to offer condolences, just in case he suspected a guilty conscience. But he had legitimate businesses and arrow-straight contacts, and it was these people who'd left messages. It was obvious that the story had leaked.

He checked Google and, sure enough, the media was all over the breaking news that a top dog gangster had lost his son to murder. That was quick. The damn police must have been falling over themselves to call journalists. Either they wanted to remind the public that Fritz wasn't an immortal god despite their failures to nab him, or they just wanted to piss him off. He didn't care about the former. The latter worked a treat.

He felt duty-bound to return the missed calls and texts, but that could wait until after he'd been to Floating Point. Leaving the city felt like abandoning Sam, but he set Jim a task and couldn't do much more than what was already in motion. Hopefully, his people would soon have a name, and upon his return to London, he could take personal charge of the final act in this tragedy: taking off a man's head with a hacksaw.

THIRTY-TWO

Running off Main Street on the Parry Estate was Barker Road, where The Ginger Ninja's best friend lived. By ten that morning word had spread, so for sure he'd know. And he might be best placed to give Fritz the information he needed.

The two heavies – brothers – that Fritz sent to his address banged on the door, which was opened by his panicked mother. Before she could utter a word, someone shouted from the top of the stairs behind her. 'Let them in, Mum. It's okay.'

The heavies pushed past her and bolted up the stairs. The teenager said, 'I know why you're here, but I wasn't with Sam last night.'

The kid probably didn't expect one claim to send them on their way, but he was taken aback when the lead beefcake grabbed a leg and yanked it out from under him. He was dumped on his ass, then dragged on it down the stairs. His mother kicked and screamed, but he remained calm.

He probably expected the interrogation to take place in their living room, but the two beefs dragged him, still by the leg, out onto the street in broad daylight, and shoved him in the back seat of a car. They got in the front, certain he wouldn't try to escape. They were right. Fritz knew where he lived.

The car turned onto Parry Street and drove alongside the crime scene. Forensics vans and two cop cars were still outside the yard round the back of the shop. It sure looked like the police might give a shit about solving this murder after all.

The car stopped at the junction, inches from the crime scene tape blocking the side road. Right where police could see it. Right where Fritz had ordered the vehicle to be paused.

Miles away from this scene, Fritz said, 'Take the camera off and let me see him.'

He was driving out of London and watching his phone, mounted on the dashboard. It showed a live feed from the driver's Axis Body-Worn Live camera. It had been fitted with bi-directional communication features, thus allowing him to talk via the device.

The image of the steering wheel jumped as the driver took the device off his chest and held it so Fritz could see the teenager. He had a hare-lip. 'See the police?' Fritz said. 'See the crime scene tape? Do you want a scene like this at your house?'

The kid looked terrified. He stared at the camera. 'There's no need for this, Mr Fritz. I wouldn't ever go against you. You ask, I do. Sam's my mate. I wasn't out with him last night. I wasn't even on the estate. The others were there, though.' He named one, who had been there to box last night. 'He'll know more. Talk to him.'

'Where's this Rocky-wannabe live? Here?'

'No, sir, about a mile away. I know the address.'

He paused. The man holding the camera said, 'What are you fucking waiting for? Mr Fritz to ask? Say the damn address. What do you think we're here for?'

The kid blurted the boxer's address. Fritz felt a little sorry for him. He'd lost a friend. He said, 'Out you get, boy. Go live a happy life. Take this gift.'

As planned, the brother playing passenger took an envelope with £1,000 from a pocket. The kid snatched it and got out of the car, right there at the police cordon. The driver helpfully turned the camera to the window, allowing Fritz to see the crime scene. A copper performing boundary security and looking bored glanced over.

'You kill the kid?' the cop yelled.

'No, man. Course not,' hare-lip bellowed back.

'Nothing to see here then, is there? Clear off. All of you.'

The kid sauntered away and the car rolled on.

THIRTY-THREE

The twenty-year-old boxing wannabe lived in an end terrace on the edge of Ickenham. It was on a commercial strip and half the terraces had been converted into shops. His front door opened onto the pavement. Fritz's two beefcakes parked right outside, but they went round the back. The rear door was unlocked and they walked straight into the house.

A woman of about ninety was in a reclining armchair in the living room, watching cartoons. She didn't even look at them, so both guys passed through and headed upstairs. No one else was present in the house. They tramped back down the stairs to ask the old dear some questions.

'Where's the kid who thinks he's hard?' was the first.

The woman jumped, as if she truly hadn't even noticed them until now. They wondered if she was senile, but her eyes were sharp and she spoke quickly.

'Good lord. What's that fool done now? To think I held him as a baby and thought he was the most special boy ever.'

'Just tell me where he is?'

'Excuse me, but where are your manners?'

These guys were brothers. They'd lost their parents early

and had been raised by a grandmother, so they had respect for elders. 'Sorry, ma'am,' the driver said. 'But I think you know he's a bit of a silly boy. He's in with the wrong people.'

'Tell me about it. Are you going to hurt him? I'm not handing him over if he's going to get hurt.'

'As long as he tells us what we need, he'll be fine.'

'You promise, young man?'

The driver said, '*I* promise not to hurt him.'

She thought. And decided. 'They're at the Beefeater on Paul Street for breakfast.'

They thanked her and left.

The Beefeater was just two minutes away. The brothers parked and walked to the entrance. The driver said, 'This kid gets tricky, you have to do the hurting.'

'Why? The hip playing up again? I told you about that acupuncture place.'

'No. I promised that granny, didn't I? Said *I* wouldn't hurt him.'

His brother laughed. 'Nice trick. Okay, I'll do it.'

They headed inside. The lunch crowd was big, but they immediately saw the table around which sat the kid they wanted, his older sister, and his parents. And immediately got spotted by their target.

As they walked over, the kid got up and started to run. His dad, also aware of the goons, yelled at him to stop. 'Where are you going, son? Spain? Are you going to live under a railway bridge? Forever? Nice knowing you.'

The Rocky-wannabe stopped. The goons reached the table. The driver snatched a piece of bacon from a plate and chewed it. The kid looked between them and his dad.

'Go on, son,' his dad said. 'Tell them what they want to know.'

The boy walked out, and the goons followed. They got him in their car. 'I know why you're here,' the kid said. 'Sam's dead.'

'Camera!' Fritz yelled. 'Brains.'

'Sorry, boss,' the driver said. As before, he unclipped the Axis bodycam and held it up so Fritz could see the interviewee. Fritz said, 'You're the second person to say you know why we came. So everyone is well aware that my boy is dead. And probably celebrating.'

The Rocky-wannabe's eyes widened as he realised who he was talking to. He tried to lean back in his seat, as if the little box spewing words might hurt him. 'Sir, no sir, Sam was my friend. I'm sad.'

'Everyone knows, yet nobody came forward. It pains me to have to chase you people down for information.'

'I didn't know that, sir. I thought you knew everything. You're the big boss of London.'

'But I'm not psychic. I need people to talk. So do that.'

'All I know is some guys came, sir. We were just all hanging out. I was having a boxing match on the grass. Some ninjas came and–'

'What?' Fritz said.

The kid nodded hard. 'Ninjas. Just like in the films. They were different colours. Three dudes. I think one was a Black guy.'

Ninjas. It sounded fanciful, but not unlikely. Sam had run a gang called The Ninja Warriors. Maybe the attackers thought it would be cool and ironic to dress as ninjas to take them down. 'What happened to my boy? They drag him off? Did they come for him specifically because of me? Was this to hurt me?'

'I don't know, sir. Didn't see. We all just legged it. I know ninjas are silly and all, but what should we have done? Three freaks came running at us. People dress like that for hitting a crew, they gotta be a bit tapped in the head. Look, sir, you need to talk to Spotter. He warned us he'd seen a dude hanging around a little bit before it kicked off.' The kid gave an address.

Fritz liked this piece of information. A dude hanging around? Must be one of the killers. 'Okay, boy. Go on back to your food. My man there is sorry for stealing that bit of bacon off your plate. Buy more with this.'

He was handed an envelope of cash, which he took tentatively. 'I'm sorry for your loss, sir. Sam was my good friend.'

'Then watch the news, because those three ninjas are going to be all over it soon.'

THIRTY-FOUR

The kid called Spotter wasn't at the address given, but two men were present. Fritz knew a bit about most of The Ninja Warriors, but not this guy, so he got his heavies to learn more from the flatmates.

Spotter had left home at seventeen and, with dreams of making it big, travelled from Edinburgh to London to start a new life. As such, the twenty-year-old had no family down south and few friends.

His flatmates knew his habits well. He was a compulsive shoplifter and liked to do his business at the Atria Watford on Sunday afternoons. The brothers got a description of what he wore and made the drive to the indoor mall. Once inside, they walked around like regular shoppers and hoped to spot him. Fritz watched it all live via the camera.

'You want me to sort this kid if he's tricky?' the passenger said to his brother.

'No,' said the driver. 'Didn't promise any grandmas about this one.'

Fritz's phone rang, interrupting the live feed. It was Jim. Fritz was annoyed. 'Busy here, Jim.'

'TGI Fridays just called the police. Non-payer who tried to run. It's Spotter according to the description.'

Fritz was puzzled and surprised – then he wasn't. Jim's ability to just *know* things was why the man was invaluable. Fritz didn't even ask how Jim had found out who they were after and where they were searching for him. 'TGI right here?'

'Right there in the Atria. And the officer dispatched is one of ours. That blonde girl with the two-legged dog. I've already briefed her on what to do.'

Jim hung up. Fritz didn't recall the officer, but the heavies did. When he imparted the information and new orders, the driver said to his brother, 'Hey, it's that one with the cute nose who you tried to chat up.'

When they got to the restaurant, they peered through the big front window and Fritz saw their man. Spotter was sitting at a corner table and three staff boxed him in. He had wiry blonde hair and wore a Covid mask. Just seconds later, a young, uniformed female police officer walked between them and the glass.

'Go to the toilets behind you,' she whispered. Fritz's video feed jumped all over the place. When it settled, he saw the wearer walking into the TGI Fridays. He realised the female officer had taken the camera and attached it to her top. Good old Jim.

The officer was approached by the manager, who gave her and Fritz the lowdown. The thief had ordered three chilli chimichangas, consumed them, and then tried to run. They'd searched him but found no money and no identification, so they called 999.

'Don't abuse 999,' she told the manager. 'Ring 101 in future. I'll take it from here and contact you when we receive payment.'

She approached the table where Spotter was boxed-in. She

asked him to remove his mask, but he shook his head. She then asked him a few questions, but he refused to utter a word.

'You're under arrest for theft,' she said. Spotter didn't react. She cuffed his hands behind his back and led him out. 'Go use the toilet before we take a ride. I don't want you peeing in my car.'

Fritz tensed. Spotter was by her side so Fritz couldn't see him. Couldn't tell if the kid was puzzled as to why a copper would order him to use the toilet before a trip to the station. But the kid still didn't say a word. She led him to the door. 'I'll have to wait out here. Female and all.'

Now he spoke. 'How do I get my dick out?'

'I'm sure someone will help. In you go.'

She'd gone too far, Fritz realised. No legit cop would let a suspect go free into a toilet in handcuffs and expect him to ask for help. Spotter had to know something was amiss. He knew something bad awaited him in the toilet. And he probably knew Fritz was its orchestrator.

Fritz knew he was right when Spotter turned to face the officer. Before the gang lord could utter a warning, Spotter drew back his head and pistoned it forwards. Fritz saw only Spotter's chest in close-up, but he heard the crunch of bone and the officer's scream.

She fell backwards, onto one side, which gave him a low down, Dutch angle as Spotter, still cuffed, ran away into the crowd. He glanced back to display blood on his forehead. Onlookers moaned and screamed and darted aside, no heroes amongst them today.

Seconds after he was gone, there was a noise: a door slamming open. The heavies, emerging from their hiding spot in the male bathroom. They appeared in shot, kneeling before the downed officer.

'Christ, look at her nose,' the passenger said. 'Guess I've gone off her.'

'Get the hell after him,' Fritz yelled. The driver grabbed his brother and they started running, hoping to spot and chase their target. Whether they would or not was not something Fritz would witness first-hand, for they neglected to retrieve the body-worn camera.

Fritz shut off the live feed.

THIRTY-FIVE

Floating Point was a two-bedroomed stone farmhouse in Minster, on the Isle of Sheppey, about fifty miles east of London. The building sat atop a low hill a hundred metres south of Minster Leas beach and was accessible via a private track running off Marine Parade. Fritz chose not to use the track and left his vehicle in a nearby car park. It was almost 4pm. He paused before entering the field, staring out across the beach and the water.

He still awaited that moment when his son's death would bust a dam and flood his mind, submerging rational thought. It was like waiting for a heart attack. Although none had been as important as Sam, he'd lost close friends to gang violence and had always gotten through the tough times by staying busy, and staying angry.

He had a killer to hunt, a wife on his case, and law enforcement breathing down his neck, and all of this should have provided enough impetus to protect him from grief.

But he was trapped between a rock and a hard place. The urge to burn energy and occupy his mind just wasn't there. Sam's death had instead instilled a desire to seek out quiet moments, but tranquillity was a fertile breeding ground for anxiety and depression. Perhaps he sought this, to hasten the arrival of that moment when reality would finally dawn. Then he would either drown, or survive and move on.

He walked up to the gate in the stone wall. He saw nobody at any of the windows. The front door was unlocked. He let himself inside and listened for a moment. No sounds. Slowly, he headed through the living room, then a kitchen in the early stages of renovation, and opened the back door. It led to a high-walled rear yard, where he found the man he'd come for.

Naked, he stood by the hot tub, tying his shoulder-length hair in a bun in preparation for entering the water. His back was to Fritz. The hot tub's loud water jets had smothered the sound of the door opening, and the noise now hid Fritz's footsteps as he crossed the yard.

Fritz got behind the muscled young man and threw an arm around his neck, locking in a chokehold.

THIRTY-SIX

The naked twenty-two-year-old man barely panicked as he was snatched in the chokehold. Fluidly, he bent forward, pulling Fritz off the floor and high onto his back.

'No, no,' Fritz moaned.

The young man ignored him. He bent forward, shook his upper body, and Fritz slipped over his head, to splash into the hot tub.

Fritz got to his feet and wiped water from his eyes. 'You twat, Josh.'

Josh folded his arms, laughing. 'You're too old, my friend. And you're late.'

Josh aside, nobody but Jim knew about this place. Marie thought he'd sold it two years ago, but he'd simply transferred it into Josh's name. Whenever Fritz visited, he always switched cars just outside London to throw off any cops that might be on his tail. His new vehicle was one unknown even to Jim. He absolutely needed to keep Floating Point his special secret. There was one very good reason for that.

'Not too old for *this*, am I?' he said, then fired out a hand

and grabbed Josh's bare junk. The boy yelped but didn't object. Fritz guided him into the hot tub with gentle tugs, where both men roughly kissed each other. Josh then helped Fritz to undress.

THIRTY-SEVEN

After using the hot tub, Fritz and Josh headed to the master bedroom. Josh was much younger and often used the gym equipment in a spare room, so he was fit and strong. He turned Fritz into a sweaty mess on the bed.

Josh did some stretching after their lovemaking. At the window was a rifle on a tripod, the barrel aimed through the glass. Fritz approached and peered through the scope. The two men liked to watch handsome, half-naked males on the beach and rate them out of ten.

Fritz wasn't game today. As soon as Josh headed for the bathroom to shower, Fritz abandoned the gun and snooped around the room. He'd met Josh eighteen months ago when he'd found the homeless young man squatting in the farmhouse. Normally such a thing would have been punished, but Josh had kept the place tidy and, God, he was gorgeous.

A deal was struck. Josh could live here, but he had to be at Fritz's sexual beck and call. That meant abandoning any kind of social life – not that he had one anyway – and remain in the farmhouse 24/7. Josh was delighted. He got free rent, free food, and he liked older men.

But the kid was so handsome that Fritz was paranoid. There was nobody here to watch him, and Fritz burned with worry that his lover might be cheating on him during the long gaps between visits. So, he snooped for clues that Josh might have another man – or woman.

Josh caught him when he returned to the room. 'Oh, you don't trust me?'

Fritz had his hands in a chest of drawers, so he could hardly deny it. 'Maybe you should be flattered.'

Josh came close, pulled those hands from the drawers, tossed away the towel around his waist, and pushed Fritz onto the bed. 'I am. But I'm also upset at your cheek, since you're cheating on me with a woman.'

'We don't sleep together. I told you that. The last time was way before I met you.'

Josh straddled him and pinned his arms down. 'Okay, I'm flattered. But when are you going to leave her?'

'Soon,' he lied. He'd love to dump Marie, but it was too big a step. He liked the married-man image he had. He knew gay gang bosses, but something about becoming known as one scared him. Did he think he'd lose respect? He wasn't sure. He just knew he didn't want to unpack his dirty laundry for everyone to see. And he didn't want the cops targeting Josh to try to turn him.

Besides, he enjoyed having a home away from home, and he loved the cloak-and-dagger secrecy.

Speaking of Marie, she rang his mobile as the men were making love again. Josh told him to ignore the call.

'Hell no,' Fritz said. 'She goes berserk if she can't get hold of me. Anyway, she might have news about...' He paused. Josh knew Sam existed. He didn't know the boy was dead, though. 'Just stay quiet while I take this.'

Marie was berserk anyway. 'Ley, where the hell are you?

Have you read the news? Have you seen what those bastards said about me?'

Yes, he'd read the news about Sam. Of course it was going to be a big story because... 'Wait, did you say about *you*?'

'Yes. I've been mentioned. A newspaper called me a chubby barmaid. How dare they!'

He stifled a laugh. 'Look, I'll be back soon. I'm following leads about Sam.'

She ranted for another two minutes, but finally he got her off the phone. Josh looked at him. 'What's up with your son?'

Fritz paused. This place was a bubble protected from everything else in his life, and he wanted to keep it that way. If he brought Sam's death here, it might taint the relationship he had with Josh. It might even erode the power this place had to ease his soul. Should he tell?

THIRTY-EIGHT

Newton picked up Louis two hours after their phone call. Sonia had gone out with the twins to a playpark. Louis invited Newton inside and the restaurateur followed him to the kitchen, where Louis sat at the table to finish a large English breakfast.

'I don't know how you can eat,' Newton said. 'I lost my appetite.'

'Same. But I don't know if I'll get chance again.'

Eat when you can was an unwritten army rule, both men knew. Newton stared at the food for a few moments, then said, 'Can I get something?'

Newton made himself sandwiches. While he buttered bread, he said, 'Told the wife the truth?'

Louis almost laughed. 'No way. I'll take that night to my damn grave. You?'

'Of course not. No wife to tell.'

'I meant did you tell anyone at all?'

'Maybe with my dying breath. I reckon you'll tell the kids about what we did.' Louis laughed, but Newton was dead serious: 'I mean it. One day, when it's old news and they're adults, you'll come clean. This won't stay buried forever.'

Perhaps not. But Louis had no confess-his-sins plans for the next couple of decades. Thinking about all this only amplified the anger he felt towards Owen. 'Let's hurry up and go see that damn idiot.'

Sandwiches made and fry-up consumed, they left the house. Standing by Newton's car, Louis pointed at the decal on the door that advertised Newton's restaurant. 'That could be risky. Got any tape?'

There was black tape in the boot. The decal was on both front doors, so they took one each. They covered the restaurant's name and address. It was a shoddy job, but adequate. 'I'll lose revenue,' Newton said.

'At least you'll live to spend what trickles in,' came the reply. They got in the car.

Newton typed Owen's postcode into his sat-nav, but didn't like what he was shown on the map. 'It's Globe Town. But it looks like an industrial estate.'

'Let's just get there and see.'

They drove. As they left Louis's estate, Newton said, 'Glove box.'

Louis opened it to find a brown envelope, which Newton said he should take and keep. Louis was shocked to see money. A lot of it. Ten thousand pounds, Newton told him. All yours.

'For what?'

'For dragging you into this.'

Louis stuffed the envelope back into the glove box. 'I chose to come.'

'Take the cash, Louis. My other offer of money was what swayed your mind and got you in this mess. You're in danger because of me. Buy the kids something good. Treat the missus. Hire a professional to hang that front garden gate correctly.'

'Sod off. It's a masterpiece, that.'

Louis didn't retrieve the envelope, so Newton reached over to take it, and dumped it in Louis's lap. 'I insist. I'm sorry that your family might be in danger.'

After another period of silence, Louis said, 'Didn't you ever want kids?'

Newton took a few seconds to consider this, his eyes never leaving the road. 'I do too many long hours. So what got you into woodworking?'

Louis realised he'd hit a nerve. He wanted to know more, but would wait until Newton offered that information. So he told Newton about his hobby.

Later they arrived at their destination. Newton turned his car into the industrial estate, which was composed of a wide main road with businesses along each side. Being a Sunday, most were shut. Nobody was around and all was quiet. Louis said, 'This is wrong. I thought maybe there'd be some flats.'

It was a no-through road. At the end, Newton turned his vehicle around and stopped. He checked the postcode Owen had written. 'Now what? Maybe he got one number or letter wrong. I'll try different ones.'

Newton started to work his sat-nav, but Louis grabbed his arm to stop him. 'Just call him. I don't want to waste time.'

Newton pulled out his phone and called Owen, who answered quickly. Newton put the call on speaker. 'That postcode you gave us is crap.'

'Postcode?' Owen said. 'You coming to see me or something?'

'Hell yes. And I bet you know why. So where the hell do you live?'

'HHS Freight Services. Just stop out front.'

Owen hung up. Newton and Louis looked at each other. The car started moving. The two men scanned both sides of the street. Soon Newton spotted it. HHS Freight Services was a decrepit, abandoned building without windows and with graffiti all over. It was a real eyesore out here amongst cleaner, active properties.

Owen emerged from behind the freight firm a few seconds later. He waved for Louis and Newton to follow, then vanished back the way he'd come. The two men got out of the car.

In the back yard of the firm was a mass of metal and wooden junk that looked like everything from inside the firm and then some. Near the back was a battered shipping container.

It was Owen's home. The guys were astounded to see that he had a sofa, a table, a foldaway bed, and a kettle, TV and lamp attached to a small generator. He'd laid a carpet and hung posters.

'I know what this is about, guys,' Owen said. He bid his pals to sit. The sofa looked like he'd rescued it from a tip and both refused. 'It's in the news. I saw.'

'Did you kill that man?' Newton said.

Owen got cans of beer from his fridge. He was the only one who wanted to drink. 'Fuck it. Yeah, I did.'

Louis asked if that had been the plan all along.

'Not the plan. But I knew he'd be there and I knew he wasn't walking away from it.'

'That sounds like a plan. You're a fucking moron.'

Newton got between the two men in case their egos took over. But Owen sat on the sofa and sipped his beer. 'How much do you care about the back story? The Ginger Ninja liked to beat the hell out of a woman I love. I decided to save her. Want any more?'

'What woman?' Louis said. 'Girlfriend?'

Owen shrugged.

'He's right, you're a moron,' Newton said. 'Do you know what shit you've put us in?'

'With Fritz or the cops?'

'Jesus. Both, you muppet. So you knew all along you were messing with fire. If we'd–'

'If you'd known, you never would have blah blah. Are you all broken up over a dead wannabe gangster?'

Louis lost it. He stepped forward and grabbed Owen's tatty tracksuit top by the chest in both hands. He yanked him to his feet. 'I'll be all broken up by a widowed wife and kids who've got no dad, you piece of shit.'

Owen closed his eyes. 'Go on. You get one shot. You deserve it. Maybe the butterfly effect will end up making all of us safe.'

Louis decided the opposite applied. Smacking this fool might ease his tension, but it would change nothing. He let Owen go and took a step back. Owen resumed his place on the sofa.

'How we feel about the man you killed isn't the issue, Owen,' Newton said.

'I'll take that as a yes. You don't care about The Ginger Ninja and neither will the cops. Trust me, there's going to be no rush to solve this one.'

'And his grieving, angry, powerful dad?'

'See that?' Owen pointed. In a corner was a pair of Asda bags for life. They brimmed with clothing.

'You're going somewhere?'

'Me and my girl are leaving shithole London. Three ninjas attacked The Ninja Warriors. No one knows who they are. I'm the only one with any sort of connection to that dead dick. Even if his dad somehow miraculously zeroed in on me, I'll be long gone. Maybe you should both get away for a bit. Louis, you said you wanted a holiday. Take it.'

'A holiday is one thing,' Newton said. 'You're running. We have lives here and can't just do that.'

Owen shrugged. 'Then stay. You'll be fine anyway. No one

will know about you guys. So chill out, okay? What's done is done. Nice knowing you. Be on your way now.'

Neither man wanted to let him off the hook so easily, but they knew nothing could be said to change anything. The damage had been done. Without another word, Newton and Louis left the container.

Back in Newton's car, Louis said, 'Think he'll tell someone about what we did?'

'It's a worry. I suppose it's good that he's leaving.'

'He was ready to fly. I bet he wouldn't have said bye if we hadn't turned up. He used us to get close to that dead kid. To kill him on purpose. He doesn't care about his old comrades.'

'I'm not about to cry that Owen Moore is no longer my good friend. So what do we do now? Answer Owen's question. Are you all broken up over a dead wannabe gangster?'

Louis thought. 'I have no plans to jump off a high bridge. I didn't kill that man. People die all the time. He chose the life. No, I'm not broken up.'

'Nor me. So we'll live our lives and survive the guilt. There's not much we can do except hope this never comes back on us. And it shouldn't as long as Owen leaves this city. And doesn't do anything stupid.'

Louis rubbed his head. 'Assuming he hasn't already.'

THIRTY-NINE

Sally answered Owen's knock with a smile that looked fake. He asked if she was okay.

'My stomach is playing up. But we're good to go. You got the money still?'

'You don't trust me?' he said.

She held out a hand. '£800.' When he paused, she added, 'You don't trust me?'

He moved past her, into the bedsit, and saw a half-packed suitcase on the floor. A good sign. 'How long until you're ready to blow this shithole?'

She shut the door, but didn't turn to face him. 'I still have some things to do.'

He held out the cash. 'Here you go. Lovely cash for my sweet baby.'

Still she faced the door, now holding her stomach with her head bowed. 'Go get your ring. It's in the bathroom.'

He went to do just that. It was on the side of the bath. He slipped it onto his finger. When he returned to the bed sitting room, Sally was still facing the door. He got a little worried. 'Are you sure you're okay? You need something for your guts?'

There was a knock at the door. One hard thump. Immediately, Sally said, 'Sorry,' and yanked it open. She fled from the bedsit.

And bumped past three large men on the doorstep. Real large. They oozed into the bedsit. One had a bat. One had a knife. One wore a pair of knuckle dusters.

Owen knew they were Fritz's men. He knew Fritz would interrogate everyone in his dead son's orbit to find his killer, and of course that would include the five prostitutes his boy pimped out.

But how much did they know? Maybe nothing yet. Maybe they were here just to interview Sally. Then again, the scene looked awfully like Sally had been waiting at the door for these brutes. And they'd just let her go.

Owen knew he was in deep shit, and he got desperate. He offered a fake smile. 'Alright, guys? Name's Ben. Enjoy the girl. I'm just heading back to the wife and kids. I don't get any off the missus these days.'

He took a step towards the door, but the guy with the knife kicked it shut. Nope, nor would Owen have fallen for such a tacky trick.

The bozo with the knuckle dusters stepped forward. Owen had both hands up close to his face. It wasn't quite a boxer's stance, but an atomic second from it. He was ready to defend himself without quite stating that. There was still a chance they knew nothing.

Knuckles pointed at the ring on Owen's finger. 'You were wrong, Owen. That symbol is not Chinese. It's kanji. And it doesn't mean happiness. It means *ninja*.'

He was also wrong about these guys. They knew a lot more than nothing.

FORTY

Josh was renovating the kitchen with a power tool when Fritz appeared in the doorway and called his name. The young man didn't hear, so Fritz approached a cable extension and yanked out the plug, killing the noise. Josh looked round.

'Take a seat,' Fritz said, pointing at the kitchen table. They sat across from each other. Josh saw the concern on Fritz's face, grinned, and said, 'I'll kill myself if you dump me.'

Earlier, Fritz had responded to Josh's question – *What's up with your son?* – with a dismissive flick of the hand. But he'd thought hard since then and decided there were some secrets that couldn't be kept.

Now, he told the tale. Josh listened with growing shock. Afterwards, he reached over the table to take Fritz's hand. 'I don't know what to say. I mean other than apologise and offer sympathy.'

Fritz nodded. 'I need revenge. I need to right a wrong. I've always been that way. But this is different. I don't know why. Part of me wants to hide in a bubble. It's strange. I've got this urge to dwell and worry because I think it will help me come to terms with it. It hasn't hit me yet.'

'The Ley I know isn't a dweller. He's a man of action, even if it's by directing that action down a phone. Don't try to change yourself. If you're confused, that's normal. You lost your son to murder. You've been knocked for six. All you can do is follow this–' Josh thumped his own chest '–and this–' He smacked his own head. 'What are they telling you?'

Fritz sighed. 'Nothing yet. I don't know what's going on. I don't know how to feel.'

'How does your wife feel?'

'She wants blood and guts. That's a little new for her, too. I mean, she's often wanted me to do someone over and sometimes for the slightest thing, but this time she's really going wild for it. But she's been losing her mind for a while now.'

'I know. Look, your head took a massive whack. Just give it time to settle, and then you'll know what you want. That's the only advice I can give.'

Fritz leaned over the table to kiss Josh's forehead. 'And that advice is good enough.'

Soon afterwards, around 7pm, Fritz set off for home. He hadn't wanted to depart from Floating Point, but everything changed when he left Minster. He seemed to pass through a kind of invisible barrier, out of ideal life and back into the real world. Best comparison: that feeling one got when the plane home touched down back home after a long and beautiful holiday.

It knocked him back on track, got his priorities in order. Now he was intent on action.

He turned off his audiobook. As he was about to call Jim for an update, the underboss rang him. 'We got one,' Jim said.

The news made Fritz's heart beat hard. They had one of Sam's killers? He didn't dare believe it? 'Who is it and are you sure?'

Jim said, 'He's a lowlife called Owen Moore. He doesn't live on Parry Estate, but he knew your son. Sam was his drug dealer. As for the part about being sure – yes. Moore just admitted the murder. He had to be tortured for it, though, so he's not in a good state. Just so you know in case you want to kill him yourself.'

Fritz no longer got involved that way and hadn't personally assaulted someone in two years. He had directly ended three lives, but those murders occurred years ago, before he got crowned king of all he surveyed.

Things were different now. The idea of using his own hands to kill Sam's murderers was sweet. But it also seemed rash and dangerous and hinted that he wasn't yet fully in control of his emotions. 'Maybe. Hold him for a bit while I think. Give him water or something. Did he say why?'

A plain and simple robbery, Jim told him. Moore was known to sleep rough and rob people for drug money. By a stroke of luck, Fritz's men visited the whores that Sam controlled and one of them had his signet ring on her finger.

'She gave Moore up, said he was coming round this evening, so I had people wait and watch. He turned up. According to her, Moore had recently got hold of some cash and was going to treat her to a night away. Our knuckles got there just in time. They found about £2,000 on him, which he claimed he'd won at a casino.'

'What about the others? You said there were three men dressed as ninjas.'

'Moore says he was alone that night. We confronted him with our evidence to the contrary, but he stuck to his story.'

'Even when bolt cutters started helping him rapidly lose weight?'

'Even then,' Jim said. 'We got his phone, but it was empty. No call logs or messages, and no contacts in the phonebook. I'll have the lads ask him again about accomplices.'

'How did this Moore know where Sam would be?'

'Well, given that Moore's mother lives on the Parry Estate, I'd say he knows the place well. So I hear, The Ninja Warriors had a regular Saturday night thing where they'd box another gang. The locals and even the police knew about it. I guess that made Sam easy to find.'

Something niggled at Fritz. He wasn't sure what it was. Something to do with the fact that Moore was a lowly dropout yet had acquired £2,000 in cash somehow. He told Jim he'd call him back and then phoned Detective Sergeant Manning, whose murder investigation team was hunting Sam's killer.

'Can't talk now, boss,' Manning said. 'I'm at the pub with my men and—'

'Get diarrhoea.'

He heard Manning tell his colleagues he needed the toilet. Footsteps. A door creaking open. 'Okay, this is what we know so far—'

Fritz interrupted again. 'I'm not calling for updates. The guy you want is already beyond your reach, so slow the horses. I want to know what my son had on him when he was found.'

House keys. Lip balm. Mobile phone. No signet ring, but apparently he always wore one. 'We think if we can find—'

'Don't waste your time looking for the ring. No wallet?'

That had been found in his flat. It was loaded with cash. 'Shall I try to get the money to you? It could be hard because—'

Sam had been a rich gang lord's son and most would assume he was flush with money. But Sam liked to force handouts, or borrow and never pay back, and that was how he paid his way. He never carried cash around. A drug customer, especially one connected to Parry Estate, would know this. So how did his scumbag dropout killer get £2,000?

Not at a damn casino, that was for sure. He hadn't sold the ring he stole, hadn't even taken Sam's phone. There could be a legitimate 'illegitimate' reason for Moore's new windfall. But Fritz was suspicious.

He knew Manning's team would have scoured Sam's phone for messages and calls and contacts. Fritz wanted every detail. Manning promised to provide the information and Fritz hung up.

He called Jim with an order. 'Go see Moore's mum. See what she knows. Find out if she gave him money, or if he stole expensive stuff from her house.'

'Wait,' Jim said. 'I sense you believe Moore didn't get the money from Sam.'

'Exactly. There's things even you don't know, Jim. Sam never carried cash around. Moore's lying about the robbery part. Maybe his mother knows the real reason he killed my son. Questioning her will raise her suspicions, so you'll be digging two graves.'

Jim understood the order, but missed the grandeur behind the words. 'One grave. We'll put them together. Easier. What about the whore? She knows we took him.'

Fritz thought. Not about whether he should end her, but of a reason why. He decided that she'd brought pleasure to his son's killer, and she'd worn Sam's ring. He said, 'Three graves.'

'No, just one, remember.'

FORTY-ONE

May Moore was in the bath that Sunday evening when two heavyset men kicked in her locked back door and ran about the house. When they appeared in the bathroom doorway, she just stared. Then she got out, and stood before them, wet and naked.

The two men were used to bust-ins that involved screaming panic. This threw them off. After a glance around to confirm there was no mobile phone in the bathroom, both stepped out and shut the door. 'Put your towel on and come out.'

She did so a few seconds later, with the towel around her waist but not over her breasts. Around her neck was a tiny perfume bottle, which she sprayed her wet chest with. The heavies didn't know where to look.

They ordered her to get dressed in the bedroom and watched through the ajar door, but only to make sure she didn't call the cops. She seemed to know they were there and faced the crack and took her time. Once she'd pulled on pants, bra, skirt and shirt, they kicked open the door. Now she was dressed, and they were in their comfort zone again.

One of the brutes slapped her hard enough to knock her onto the bed. Usually, if it was a woman they dealt with, a rape threat would get things moving along nicely. They figured this babushka might just willingly take the ride.

So, they showed her a knife, and it did the trick. The woman exited her dreamlike state and got with reality. She finally realised she was in trouble. She tried to scream, but a hand muffled it. Once she'd calmed down, or at least stopped struggling, it was time for some very important questions.

'What's with all the dolls downstairs?' one guy said.

His pal brushed that aside. 'Your son did something bad on this estate yesterday. We know you know something about it. So tell us a little story, and this one might have a happily-ever-after ending for you.'

He liked that line. He'd used it many times. And it always worked.

The 'story' was passed to Jim, who called Fritz with a condensed version. 'You won't believe this. Get ready. Half the people on Parry Estate are involved. They set it up. They wanted something done about the troublemaking, so Ms Moore asked her son for help. They paid him. That's where he got the money.'

Fritz was on the last leg of his journey home from Floating Point. He pulled up at a kerb to take the remainder of the call. 'And he had help?'

'Moore used to be in the army. He got some old friends in on the action. So that confirms what we heard about there being three men dressed as ninjas. But Ms Moore claims the Parry Estate residents only wanted the gang scaring off. I believe that. It appears Moore went overboard, or he took it upon himself to kill Sam. He was always having run-ins with your boy, usually over money owed.'

'Did she have any more names for us?'

'No,' Jim said. 'She swears to God – literally – that she doesn't know who he recruited. I don't see why she'd protect them if she knew. It took her a New York Minute to admit her son's involvement and nobody had hurt her at that point. She even said she'd bless us if we got rid of him. It seems she's a wee bit embarrassed by her offspring.'

'We'll grant that wish. But after we have another chat with him.'

Fritz hung up. When he got home, one of his live-in security exited their office and said, 'Okay, boss?'

Actually, he was. He'd made vital progress in his hunt for Sam's killers. It felt good to be active and achieving, just like old times. He'd made the right decision by opting not to dwell and pause. If there was a bomb-blast of grief heading his way, maybe it would wait until after he'd avenged his son. He'd happily deal with it then.

'Where's my wife?' he asked the security guard.

'Out, but I'm not sure where she went.'

Fritz headed into the kitchen. He decided not to call Marie because he wanted none of her vitriol. He discovered that she'd left one of her unfunny joke messages for him. A Post-it note on the fridge said, *Your dinner's in here.* He looked and there was nothing prepared. Ha fucking ha.

Normally he didn't shower after sex with Josh because the man-stink would convince Marie he didn't have another woman. But right now he felt he needed to soak. He ran a bath, lay back, and played an audiobook on the TV mounted on the wall.

He couldn't concentrate on it, though. One man had been found, but three had attacked his son's gang. It didn't matter if Moore alone stabbed Sam. Joint enterprise. They all had to die. The job was only a third complete.

But the blame wasn't confined to a trio of fools dressed as ninjas, was it? There were others without whose input Sam would still be drawing breath. Fritz lobbed the TV remote away and grabbed his phone. Jim answered within three seconds, as always.

'The people of Parry Estate wanted peace and quiet,' Fritz said. 'It's unfair for them to find benefit from another's misfortune.'

Jim understood. 'How extreme?'

'They should live to regret it.'

In other words, go to town, but kill no one. Ten seconds after Fritz hung up, Jim was on another call. In a house on the outskirts of London, a man took that call and set off a rape alarm. A bit over the top, but it was his way of alerting the six other men in the property that it was go-time.

This was Fritz's rapid response – or hit – squad. Seven men, awaiting an order to strike. They were trained badboys, but Fritz didn't run a Mexican drug cartel and they'd grown rusty on standby.

One guy panicked and claimed to have a bellyache. Another guy cursed the gods because he'd just sat down for a shit. A third moaned because he was on a time-challenge on a mobile phone game. The van needed petrol. Nobody knew where the key to the weapons cupboard was. The man who took the call from Jim had to return it because he'd forgotten the target's postcode.

But they got their arses in gear and eighty minutes after the order came, a bland and windowless and utterly untraceable van rolled into Parry Estate.

FORTY-TWO

Around ten that evening, Newton called Louis, who was out in his shed and crafting pieces for a chessboard. He'd also hidden the envelope containing ten grand there. The restaurateur was very agitated. 'Fritz's men just hit Parry Estate.'

He told a story in rapid, short sentences, and Louis missed most of it. He had to order his friend to slow down. He headed into the back yard when he heard Sonia coming downstairs from the toilet.

Newton composed himself and retold it. Louis believed every word, but he hung up the call and checked online newspapers to make sure Newton wasn't wrong. He wasn't. The story was everywhere, and had even made national news.

Parry Estate, village of Ickenham, borough of Hillingdon, had tonight been the scene of horrendous carnage. Six masked men entered the estate, and then entered houses. They had bats. They had knuckle dusters. They had hydrofluoric acid in little balloons made from the fingers of chemically resistant gloves.

Residents settled on their sofas or in their beds were attacked at random. Skin was lacerated, flesh was burned, bones were broken. Property was smashed to pieces. Twelve homes were invaded, but at twenty-two additional residences, no entry was made but windows were busted. Additionally, the van that brought the men was pinballed around the estate, smashing into or scraping alongside nineteen vehicles, four of which were write-offs. The van was found on fire a mile away.

After that invasion came one by emergency services. As of writing, twenty-three people were in hospital. Two dozen officers were asking questions of those who'd been lucky enough to escape the carnage. It was early into the investigation, but already police had a motive. Unbelievably, the van driver had blurted it through a megaphone as the attackers got in their busted van and drove away: 'Don't fuck with the wrong people.' And: 'This has been fun. Same time next week, eh?'

No one was in doubt. This was payback for the death of Sam Fritz, son of London's king ne-er-do-well, on their turf.

Louis called Newton back. Both men had the same thing on their minds: Fritz knew the residents had paid people to confront The Ninja Warriors. But how?

'Owen's mum,' Louis said. He didn't want to face the other possibility.

Newton wasn't so reserved. 'Or Owen himself. I called him, Louis. His phone is dead.'

Louis said it might be the battery, or it could be busted, or Owen got rid of the device because he was skipping town. He believed none of his own logic, however. He had to face the stark reality that somehow Fritz had found Owen and tortured the tale from him.

'But why haven't we been targeted?' Newton said. 'Owen came to your house. He knows where you live.'

Louis left the shed and moved around the side of that same house, to stand at the front and scan the street. The people of Parry Estate weren't a fraction as guilty as him, so surely he would have been a more important target. But no van of masked men was on the street. 'Owen must not have told Fritz anything. We might have this wrong. Maybe he's okay.'

'Well, we can't take that risk, Louis. What happened on Parry Estate wasn't just Fritz venting at the place where his kid got whacked. But nobody died. If there's a plan for murder, maybe it's waiting for the dead of night.'

Newton's words chilled him, even though he'd been thinking the same thing. 'What can we do? Hide?'

'I can. I'm going to sleep at a hotel tonight. I'll put you up in the same one if you want. You and the wife and the kids. You can tell Sonia I booked an extra room by mistake and it shouldn't go to waste.'

'No. She'd know something is up because it's so last minute. And then what about the day after? If Fritz knows about us, one night away isn't going to help.'

'Okay, Then how about I come to yours? Just in case. Army of two.'

Having Newton at his home overnight would be akin to admitting there was a threat, and Louis didn't want to do that. But he agreed to the plan because what he wanted even less was to be woken at 3am and realise he should have been more pessimistic.

FORTY-THREE

A gas leak. Newton's house was getting aired out and he needed a place to stay, so Louis had offered his own for a night.

'No, I'm not going to lie to my wife,' Louis said. Rather than use Newton's excuse, he would simply tell Sonia that his friend wanted to stay over. 'I mean, that's true, right? You want to stay at mine, don't you?'

Newton grinned at him. 'Still seems deceptive.'

'But not a lie.'

Sonia was happy to allow a friend of Louis's to spend the night. She reminded him that he needed more time with men outside of work.

Newton arrived with just the clothing on his back. He scanned the street for bad guys as he walked up the path. Louis met him at the door with a warning to stay calm in case Sonia noticed something amiss.

'I reckon we're safe anyway,' he added. 'Something would have happened to us already if Owen gave us up. Remember, we deleted all calls and messages, so his phone won't tell them a thing. Maybe they never even got to him. He could be dead by overdose in a crack den.'

Newton said, 'You really think that?'

'I'm trying to.'

Sonia met Newton and the three of them stayed up and talked until midnight, when Sonia retired to bed. She had an early start at work on Monday for a stocktake.

That left the boys alone. They tried to act casual and talked of things unrelated to Owen and gangs and dead young men, but there was a tense air. They tried to watch TV, but Louis kept muting it every time he heard a sound from beyond the living room.

'Paranoia?' Newton said.

'Just being careful.'

Louis noticed that Newton still had his shoes on. 'Paranoia?'

'Just being careful,' Newton said.

Louis put on his own footwear. Soon after, he got an apple to eat and cut it with a large steak knife, which he left on the coffee table. Newton eyed it suspiciously.

'Yep, paranoia,' Louis said.

'Fuck it. Just in case, eh? What else can we do?'

The window was left ajar, so they could hear any cars or pedestrians that approached the house. Newton put a garden fork by the front door and Louis left a spade by the kitchen exit. Each man typed 999 into their phones, ready to summon help with one button. Louis also brought his son's baseball bat downstairs, an item he had hewn from a block of wood.

Newton hefted it. 'If this was yellow, I'd try peeling it.'

'Get lost. The wood warped in the heat.'

They decided to sleep in two shifts, so somebody would always be awake. At least, that was the plan. Neither man managed much sleep. Around 2am, Newton said, 'Did you tell Sonia about the money I gave you?'

'No. It's hidden. I thought I'd bring it out piecemeal. Is that silly?'

'She might think you're dealing drugs. Just tell her it's a gift from me for old times' sake. A present for saving my life that day. Remember? The Challenger 2?'

Louis did. In Afghanistan in 2001, a tank had almost run Newton down, but Louis had yanked him out of harm's way. 'But you bought me a pint for that.'

'Buy another with the money. But tell your wife.'

By 5am, both men were sitting up, wide-eyed. But they also began to relax. The birds were chirping and the new day seemed to have arrived. At seven, Newton clapped his hands together. 'Well done us. Another night survived. Still alive.'

When Sonia woke, both men put their brave faces on. They laughed and joked with her until she'd left for work. The day was bright, which helped ease more tension. Until Newton called Owen again but got nothing.

'We need to talk to him, or know what, if anything, had happened to him.' Louis said. 'Until then it's going to be hard to just get on with my damn life.'

'Ditto. If we haven't heard by tonight, what do we do? The hotel idea? Now Sonia's got time to get ready for it.'

He hoped it wouldn't come to pass. But he agreed to ask her.

FORTY-FOUR

Seven hours earlier, as midnight approached, Marie made a snack in the kitchen and was uncommonly quiet. Fritz thought nothing of it and didn't question her when she said she was going out to see a friend. Nor did he see anything amiss when, half an hour later, his phone rang.

It was Jim. 'I heard of a call to the police about a woman matching your wife's description at a house on Shallow Road. She forced her way into—'

'Shit,' Fritz said. 'I'm going there. Try to delay the police somehow.'

Shallow road was near Barnet Hospital, some thirty miles away. It could be a long drive if traffic was heavy. Fritz made it in an hour, but that wasn't good. He expected the police to be in attendance and they were. But he saw just one car with two officers inside. Nothing seemed amiss about the standard semi on this urban street. It was after the dead of night and quiet.

The officers watched as he parked and walked up the garden path, but they didn't emerge or try to speak to him. He knocked and the door was opened by a middle-aged man, who immediately said, 'Are you the husband? She's upstairs.'

The man stepped aside and Fritz, without word, entered and climbed to the first floor. He knew which room Marie would be in.

The smallest back bedroom was quite different to how he remembered it. He'd last been here perhaps seventeen years ago, when the walls had been covered in X-men posters. Now it was an office.

Marie stood at the window, staring at her own reflection in the dark-blackened glass. 'I paid them,' she said. She turned for a second, just to look at him, and he saw eyes wet with tears. 'The owners. To tell the police it was a misunderstanding.' Back went her eyes to the window. Normally Marie exhibited frustration and depression and sorrow by exposing volatile anger. This demeanour seemed alien, but then again she'd never before lost a son.

'Why did you come here?'

'At times I wish I'd stayed here. This was a safe space.'

How could he argue with that? Hadn't he just been to a playpark for the same reason? This was Sam's former bedroom, where there had been nothing but fun and tranquil times.

When he and Marie had started dating, she had of course known who he was. She had loved the money – he had thrown it at her, allowing her to spend willy-nilly. She had loved the clout – it erased queues in shops and everybody suddenly got more respectful. And she had loved the notoriety – her friends got bored with endless tales of his criminal and intimidatory behaviour.

But she had also been well aware that his power was something the trolls lurking under bridges wanted to strip away. Despite being well-known as his girl, once Sam was born, she had refused to sleep by his side in case someone tried to kill him in the dead of night. He understood this and often got his head down at different places. So for the first eighteen years of their boy's life, she had lived right here in this house and Fritz had visited when he could.

Only when Sam became an adult and moved out did she finally want to move in with him. Fritz was also tired of the hobo-like existence and bought the house in Kilton Park. Sam had only visited it a handful of times.

And now Marie was back here, pulled by reminders of happier times. He didn't know how to feel about that. For the past few years her head had been going crazy and it had become the new norm. He was discomfited by these rare moments when she showed a human and damaged soul without spitting venom. But at least it was a positive product of her grief instead of snarling rage.

He wondered where his heart might be if this version of Marie had always been the dominant one. Would he have sought comfort with another man?

As if she'd read his mind and was determined to set him straight, she punched the window hard enough to crack it. It made her knuckles bleed, but she shook the hand and sprayed blood droplets onto the glass. 'Why have you come here? Leave me in peace. You're wasting time. My son's killers are out there and you're standing here feeling sorry for yourself.'

Without word, Fritz turned for the door.

FORTY-FIVE

Around 7am, Fritz was knocked out of sleep by his ringing phone. Marie snored beside him, so he headed into the hallway to take the call. It was from Sergeant Manning, and it was bad. His son's phone was empty of messages, calls, and contacts. It seemed Sam committed everything to memory.

Fritz had taught him that. If the cops got the phone, they couldn't trace cohorts or see criminal plans. The killer, Moore, also had a sterile mobile because his world was similarly comprised of scumbags.

Manning said his team had hounded Sam's network provider for a list of the calls and messages, but it could be a slow process.

'Because who gives a toss about my son, right?'

Manning started to trip over his denial, and Fritz hung up on him. He could get Jim to find someone who could access the data, and that on Owen Moore's mobile, but that, too, would take time. Besides, if Moore had been smart, he wouldn't have discussed murderous plans with his ninja cronies by phone. Even if he had, they might have used untraceable burners.

If the trail ran dead cold, Fritz might set that in motion, but right now it didn't seem worth the output.

He went back to bed, certain he wouldn't sleep. He managed to drift in an out, and he was awake at 6am when Marie got up. A few minutes after she'd dressed and gone downstairs, his attempt to sleep was disturbed by his ringing phone. It was Jim. He put it on speakerphone and left the device on the bedside table.

'Owen Moore is one callous bastard,' Jim said.

He went on to explain that Moore had stuck to his me-only story even though he'd been tortured right alongside his elderly mother. Bleeding and in pain, she'd demanded of her son to come clean and give the names of his partners-in-crime. But Moore had steadfastly denied that he'd worked with a team.

The mother had died of her injuries within an hour, but Moore had held on all night, until speech was impossible. And now he would never speak again. 'Apologies for that. I know you wanted the *coup de grâce*. Do you want to watch the burial? Or throw the first clod of earth? It's happening soon.'

Jim was right. Fritz had wanted to deliver the killing blow while staring into Moore's eyes. But he found he didn't really care that the chance had been snatched away. The man was dead and about to go in the ground. 'What am I, chief mourner? Just get rid of the bodies. Any of the Parry Estate people say anything?'

Jim said that he'd had people make untraceable phone calls through the night and this morning, promising immunity to anyone who could offer names. Most had denied being part of the scheming cabal. A few were sorry about what had happened, but couldn't help. More of Sam's social circle had been interrogated, to no avail. Still they couldn't locate the missing man called Spotter, who'd escaped capture in the shopping centre.

'Get pressure on his parents,' Fritz said.

'No can do. Spotter has no local family. They're in Scotland, but he's excommunicated, hasn't had anything to do with them for years. I believe he once told someone it was because he killed the family dog. He's got no one.'

Shit. 'Okay. Keep me informed.' When Fritz killed the call, he turned to see Marie standing in the doorway with a plate of eggs on toast. His favourite breakfast. He must have done something to heighten her mood. But he never got to taste it. Her face darkened and she threw the plate at him. Egg splattered his chest and the plate ricocheted off his shoulder, to smash against the wall.

'What the fuck?' he yelled, slapping hot oil off his skin.

'"Okay"? Just "keep me informed"? If we need this man called Spotter to find my son, then you damn well do it, Ley. You owe me a head.'

He didn't have the energy to argue. 'What shall I do?'

'Find Spotter's family in Scotland. He must still care about them. Find someone vulnerable. If he's got a little sister, make her Amber Alert material. When Spotter finds out she's missing, he'll know you did it. And he'll crawl out from under his little rock.'

A terrifying idea. Over the line. Beyond his moral scope. But not beyond Marie's, and he was in no mood to loiter on her bad side today. So he smiled, told her, 'That's a great plan, thank you,' and called Jim with the most outrageous order he'd ever given.

FORTY-SIX

In the end, no child kidnapping was necessary. After Fritz had given the order, Marie mellowed and offered to make him eggs on toast again. But it required a trip to the little shop up the road, which she put on him. He threw on a T-shirt but kept the tracksuit bottoms he often slept in.

When he left the gated compound in his car, a young man stepped out of the bushes near the guard shack. Damn blind security guard. Fearing an attack, he hit the gas and blew away. In his rear-view, he saw the man in the tree-lined road, waving. Something about him was familiar.

The hair did it for him. Fritz turned his car in the road and drove slowly back. The kid was now on the side of the road, and on his knees. Fritz stopped alongside, but on the far lane just in case he had this wrong, and buzzed his window down. 'Get in.'

The kid entered the car, but tentatively. As soon as the door was shut, Fritz drove. 'Well done for finding my house. You have some skills. You're the one they call Spotter.'

The kid nodded. 'I'm sorry, sir. I know you've been looking for me. I wanted to come straight to you and apologise. I know I've wasted your time. I'm so sorry.'

'Just talk, kid. Give me something good and that will be end-of-story. I won't hurt you. In fact, given how you didn't run to the cops and managed to hide for two days, maybe I'll pay you to work for me. If your info is good. I'm looking for the men who killed my son, as you well know. Right now, give me something.'

'I wasn't at the estate. I was on the edge, spotting for cops, so–'

'Stop. I don't want your excuses. Don't make me ask again. Just give me something. I heard that you saw a man near the estate that night.'

'Yeah. I went off the road and into the trees to take a piss. A dude walked past. I heard that the men were dressed as ninjas, but not this dude. He was just normal. Black guy. But he had something called Fodder written on his car. I saw that.'

'What's Fodder?'

'Well, the advert also had a picture of a restaurant. So I guess it's one of those. So, I don't know if that dude was one of the ninjas, but he was there that night. That's all I know, sir. I'm sorry. I would have come forward straight away if I knew he was one of them. I was scared.'

Fritz stopped the car. He slapped the steering wheel in anger. Spotter freaked out and spewed apologies. 'Calm down, Spotter. Your info is handy. Now, I need one more favour from you. Are you up for it?'

A soft nod. Fritz knew the kid was worried he'd be given a nasty task. Or he feared a trick. Fritz's car wasn't a flashy, expensive vehicle, so he couldn't be fully certain his brains wouldn't be painted across the upholstery. Maybe he thought Fritz would pull out a gun and say, *The favour is, please die in agony*. It made the gangster smile. It had been a long time since a man had cowered before him.

Fritz pointed past Spotter, out the window. 'See that shop? I forgot my wallet. Go in there and steal me some eggs.'

FORTY-SEVEN

At the northern end of Chingford and running through the southern part of Epping Forest was a very apply named strip of tarmac. Bury Road. It was here that the men tasked with the disposal of three corpses decided to get out their spades. It happened at just after six in the morning.

Three men worked hard and fast, then called back their driver. As soon as he pulled up, all four men got the three bodies out. This was where it went wrong.

Jim had ordered one grave, but, still missing the point, he'd moaned that Fritz had wanted three. The trio of diggers hadn't been sure what to do, so they stopped after they'd dug two.

The problem was that they'd originally aimed for three, so each hole was deep enough for only a single corpse. Owen, the biggest, got one all to himself. The sex worker and Owen's elderly mother had to share and were stacked. There was a quite-adequate foot of earth atop Owen, but only three inches of soil lay on May Moore's back.

When a trucker stopped for a piss nearby, the diggers abandoned the duty of piling woodland detritus atop the graves and recalled their driver.

If there had been a world record for the quickest discovery of a buried body, it got broken that morning. Eighteen minutes after the last shovel of dirt was cast, a dog walker found his puppy Labrador digging away. He saw a flowery skirt. Roses are red, but so were these daisies.

He called in the police, who quickly located two dead women and a fresh mound of earth right by it. Forty minutes later, the place was heaving with living bodies. With no time to decompose, two of the dead offered perfect fingerprints.

The elderly lady wasn't in the system, but police got a hit on Sally Monroe, twenty-four, known sex worker. The male had no fingers, so no prints, but a bobby manning the cordon caught a glance of his face and, past the bludgeoning it had received, recognised him. Police visited the only address he'd ever been registered at – his mother's – and found it empty, but with signs of a struggle. That gave them a pretty good idea of the identity of the dead pensioner.

Not until much later would members of the public be informed of the vile discovery, unless you were a man with dozens of police officers in your pocket. Murder Investigation Team Six was still on call for the week, so Sergeant Manning made a phone call while his people were still umming and ahing at the deposition site.

'Are you fucking joking?' Fritz yelled down the phone. He was in his back yard, alone, enjoying the greenery and trying to kill impatience-fuelled anxiety. Moore's mother was from Parry Estate and only an imbecile wouldn't connect her death with recent events there. Playing it safe, Fritz assumed there were some non-imbeciles in the Metropolitan Police and got hold of Jim.

'I heard, of course,' Jim said. 'This will come back on you. That's another arrest, probably.'

'I bloody know,' Fritz moaned. 'We need... what's the word? A scapegoat.'

'Patsy.'

'Whoever. Offer him a deal.'

Jim laughed. He was strict and straight and severe, but now and then the strangest moments could offer mirth. 'No, a patsy. It means the same as scapegoat. A fall guy.'

'So why change my word if scapegoat will do?'

'Whatever. We can use The Hammer. An extra twenty won't bother him.'

'Good. Do it.'

'Consider it done.'

Fritz was in no mood for any crap from anyone. 'It's not done, though. Unless it is? Did you see the future and arrange it all already? Maybe I should consider myself dead because it'll happen in the next fifty years.'

'Consider it getting done right now,' Jim said, showing a rare sliver of his own anger, and hung up.

Mark 'The Hammer' Hinds was in HM Belmarsh, doing a life sentence with a thirty-seven-year-minimum. He was eleven years into it. He'd also been given a second life sentence two years ago, for a murder orchestrated from behind bars.

But he'd orchestrated nothing. The second murder had been committed by Fritz's people. Hinds was happy to remain in prison until they carried him out in a box, and if he could obtain luxuries by taking the blame for another's endeavours, so be it. Fritz needed him again.

Jim worked quickly and called back within an hour. He said he'd gotten word to The Hammer, who had access to secret phones in prison. 'I got a man to call in a tip to Sergeant Manning. Tip man will go on record saying he heard that The Hammer ordered the hit on Moore, the whore, and his mother.'

'That sounds like a film title.'

'The Hammer is being given some background on Moore. When police question him, he'll admit he ordered the hit because Moore stuffed one of his men on a drug deal. The whore was in on it. The hitmen found them at the mother's house, so she was collateral damage. With The Hammer ready to close a triple kill file, the police won't dig too deep.'

Fritz relaxed. 'Payment?'

'The Hammer's daughter could do with a new car, he says. There's some loud students living next door to his wife. Oh, and her shed's falling apart.'

Taking the piss or what? 'Okay. Take the girl shopping. Slap the students. Fix the shed.'

'Consider it being done at the moment.'

Fritz laughed. He wasn't sure he'd get too many more amusing moments over the coming days, weeks, years. He needed a break from all this hassle.

Jim was adept at problem solving, but also a master at delivering bad news. 'The story of Moore's murder will come out. The other members of Moore's killer gang will do the maths and know we're onto them. Is it wise to wait until tonight to hit the Fōda restaurant?'

'That's when the most staff will be present.'

'Perhaps we could burst in right now and find the employee via the staff files.'

'No. There's no guarantee the Black guy's file is there. He might not even work for them. We wait and do it the way I said.'

'The Moore story will break way before tonight. If his partners hear it, they might go to ground before we can find the Black guy.'

Fritz was bored of this chat now. 'The ground is exactly where they're going, my friend,' he said, and hung up.

FORTY-EIGHT

Ever since Operation Kickass, Newton had found a new energy reserve. On Monday afternoon he was at Fōda, in Hammersmith. One of his staff was due a final written warning. He buzzed with the need to move, be active, burn kilojoules. He sat the twenty-six-year-old Black man at his desk and paced while he talked about the core values of compassion, contribution, and community.

Allen seemed to not care. He'd worked security at the restaurant for eight months, and it was the first job he'd had since leaving school. Newton had taken a chance on him, but regretted it now. The kid couldn't stop being rude to customers. But a boss had to be professional.

However, when something he said elicited a tut, Newton decided he'd had enough. He kicked Allen's chair. 'Get up.'

He did. He was tall, big, strong-looking. In a marathon, he'd have the older guy all day long. But how about a sprint?

'You want to punch me, right?'

The employee thought about it. 'That would get me fired.'

'It's coming soon, I can guarantee you that. But you'd punch me if you could get away with it?'

Another little think. 'Maybe.'

'Go for it. One in the stomach. If I make a noise, you can have a guaranteed job for the next five years. But I get a punch, too. You make a noise, you're gone right now.'

The employee looked him up and down, and said *no*. It satisfied Newton. He gave the man a final written warning and told him to get back to work.

His next task was to drop in at his other restaurant for a staff budget meeting, but he didn't fancy it. Stuffy car, London traffic, yet another manager sucking up to him. He knew what he wanted to do instead. Owen's lack of contact was worrying. There could be a simple reason, but he needed to know. He was his own boss. He could come and go as he wished. And he wished to get the hell out of here.

He called Louis, who was at home and shaving ready for his evening shift.

'Call in sick. Get a bellyache,' Newton told him.

'That's for kids. It would be a viral condition.'

'A joke robbed right out of *Only Fools and Horses*. Just get something. In fact, quit that shit. Call your boss right now. Is he a twat?'

'First order dickhead. Didn't pay me when one of my little ones was ill last month.'

'Then don't even call. I'll employ you at one of my hat stalls. I've got four and one is in Hounslow. You just sit there playing on your phone and sell a hat here and there. You've got my ten grand to tide you over. Told the missus yet?'

'No. And what are we doing if I call in sick?'

Newton told him he wanted to find Owen. Maybe his shipping container home held a clue as to where he'd gone with his girlfriend. 'We need to downgrade or go to DEFCON 1. This sitting in the middle bit is making me antsy. I need to know what's going on.'

'So do I,' Louis said. 'So come get me. We've got a babysitter who watches the kids until Sonia gets back about half six, but I can get her to pick the kids up from school as well.'

'So you'll call the boss?'

'He'll realise come five o'clock when I don't turn up. But I'll tell Sonia. She can do more damage to me.'

Newton was at his door forty minutes later. They drove to Owen's 'home'. The industrial estate was in the midst of a working day and they waited for a quiet moment to slip around the back of the non-operational freight firm. A couple of teenaged boys were playing in the shipping container. They panicked upon seeing moving shadows and then two men blocking their exit.

'Calm down, boys,' Louis said. 'We're land security. We heard someone lives here. That's trespassing. Know anything?'

'No,' one said. 'We just found it. We haven't stolen anything. We won't.'

Owen had left everything behind, which meant he probably planned to return. Louis and Newton got the kids out of there, warned them never to return, and shut up the container. The box was distorted and the doors wouldn't fully close, so they used junk to hold the metal flaps in place.

As they were leaving, Newton said, 'Fingerprints. The police might come.'

It felt like overkill, but they took no chances. They found old rags and wiped down the container's doors and the junk they'd handled. Out on the road, Newton found another fault with their visit to Owen's home. CCTV cameras from the other businesses would have captured them heading around the back of the freight firm. Maybe also the numberplate of Newton's car.

Louis said, 'You burn the buildings on the left and I'll take the right.'

It was a joke, but none of this was a laughing matter. Newton was now eager to hit another location. 'Parry Estate.'

'Why?'

'Owen's mother might know something. And maybe we can get some vibes from the area.'

It was the lion's den and Louis wanted to stay clear. But Newton was right. And a deep part of Louis fancied returning to ground zero.

When they drove onto Main Street, both men got a shock. They knew about the attack on Sunday, but seeing the aftermath was a level up. Glass still glinted on the streets and the windows it had come from were boarded over. The shop looked as if it had had a new window. Almost every car against the kerbs had some kind of damage. The 'vibe' was distress.

'We might stand out being here,' Louis said. 'Let's get gossip from the shop. And use house number 26 there.'

They parked outside the shop and exited the car. Louis took Newton's hand, which got no objection beyond a strange look. They went in. The fifty-something shopkeeper, in a shirt that strained around his large belly, asked what they were looking for. He eyed the men warily, especially their clasped hands.

'We're thinking of moving down here to London,' Louis told him. 'We saw that number 26 is for sale. We just wanted to get a feel for what the area is like. Did you have an earthquake or something? All that damage. Shocking.'

The shopkeeper snorted derisively. 'This place is hell on earth. You'd hate it.'

'What happened?'

'Everything. Everything that's bad. A gang kid got killed in my back yard. He had the flat upstairs. Now his dad's pissed at us all and his men trashed every house. But the cops can't do anything. An old lady went missing yesterday, and her son's a waster drug addict. Some young thug keeps stealing...'

Newton and Louis zoned him out as they looked at each other. Newton asked about the lady. Run away? Kidnapped?

'Who knows. Not like her, though. Never leaves the house normally. Probably something bad. Cops were round there earlier with the crime vans and all. But they won't tell us a dime.'

Newton asked her name – just in case they heard anything on their travels and could help. When the shopkeeper uttered the words 'May Moore,' the two men squeezed each other's hand.

The shopkeeper wasn't done ranting. 'So just about every place will be up for sale soon. Probably get one for twenty quid. But, trust me, you won't want it. Idiots everywhere. Anyhows, your kind wouldn't fit in too well.'

'Gays or blacks?' Newton said. They didn't wait around for an answer.

FORTY-NINE

Driving out of the estate, Newton said, 'They got Owen.'

'I know,' Louis said.

They sat in silence for half a mile. Newton broke it. 'We don't know how much they know.'

'I know.'

'We can't take the risk that all the bad guys are throwing a party because they got their man.'

'I know.'

'I reckon we need to clear out of the city for a while. Owen might be giving the wrong people our names right now.'

Again, Louis knew. Newton pulled into a bus stop. His hands were shaking. 'Have you got any plans? Somewhere you can go?'

'I haven't got past thinking of how I'm going to tell my wife that I fucked up our lives. She's not going to love becoming Mrs Smith and living in Guernsey. What's the phone number for Witness Protection?'

'I don't think it's called that. And we'd probably get a cell because that gangster's kid got killed. Look, I don't–'

A bus blared its horn. Newton got moving before

continuing what he was saying. 'I don't have your problems, Louis. Wife, kids. But wives and kids need holidays, and you said the missus is craving a break away. I've got a static caravan in Cleethorpes.'

Louis looked at him. His mind had been wandering, but he got it on track. 'That could work. A week or two on holiday wouldn't look suspicious.'

'I can pay for everything. I'll pay missed wages. I'll pay any charge for taking the kids out of school. You can tell Sonia that these two weeks are the only free ones I have.'

Louis liked it. Two weeks would tell the tale. Ley Fritz was desperate to avenge his son and had already made violent progress. He wouldn't sit on his heels. If no one had come for them in a fortnight's time, it might never happen.

'Take me home,' Louis said.

Newton drove fast, as if a threat on Louis's home was imminent. As he was approaching the front door, his phone rang. His boss. It was 4.52pm. He killed the call and put on his serene face to thank the neighbour for her babysitting duties. He told her he wasn't at work that evening, gave her £10 for picking up and watching the kids, and sent her on her way.

The kids were upstairs. He told them they were going somewhere special on holiday. When? Right now. They whooped with glee and started dragging clothing out of drawers. Louis told them not to bother because they'd buy new apparel once they were settled into their caravan. He also told them the school had cleared them for take-off. The kids needed no more convincing.

After collecting the hidden envelope of cash, he led them to the car, where they greeted Newton with fist-bumps and fought over the seat behind Louis, so they could watch Newton driving. Louis settled it with a flipped coin.

'Are we getting mum?' Theo said.

'Yes, right now.'

'Is she as happy as us about it?' Louise asked.

Louis didn't want to lie, so he said nothing. When Newton jabbed a button that opened a monitor in the back of the centre console so the kids could watch TV, they quickly forgot all about their mother's happiness.

FIFTY

The police loved and loathed gangland funerals. The turnout was usually a who's who of local villains, which was good news for gaining intel and maybe snaring a wanted man. The bad was that protestors and rivals attended and trouble usually kicked off.

Sam Fritz was one such gangster, but he also had a father in the upper echelons of organised crime. The police expected hundreds and the rumours were that they would get it. There would be a carriage drawn by black horses. Ten limos would follow it. Fritz had pre-booked a church and 300 people were due to attend. He'd put a deposit down on a small plane to fly a banner and would launch thousands of pounds worth of fireworks.

The police were already checking out the church grounds for the best places to hide plainclothes officers with video cameras. As for when the funeral would take place: unknown. The coroner hadn't yet released the dead man's body.

The police would waste their time. Fritz had made these arrangements in order to throw the police and his haters off.

The grieving couple planned to have a small funeral and invite only a handful of their closest friends.

That Monday afternoon, Fritz and Marie were in Oxted, Surrey, looking at headstones in the back room of a funeral parlour. It was a depressing place. The headstones were lined up like dominoes, dozens of them. It was like a graveyard itself.

'Black?' she said, pointing at a collection in that colour.

Fritz shrugged.

'Shall we just throw Sam's body in a ditch?' Marie was annoyed at his seeming lack of care. And care he really didn't, but not because he wasn't torn up about his son's death. Something seemed wrong about shopping for a headstone. Who was it for? Sam, to show they cared? Or for his grieving parents, so they'd have something physical to replace him?

The same went for a grave. People didn't want to let go, that was why they buried their dead and created monuments. He suddenly didn't like the idea of it. How many gravestones had he helped sell?

Marie nudged him and demanded an answer. She actually wanted a response to her stupid question.

He said, 'No, of course not. I just meant I think you should pick. You know best.'

It was a line he'd used before and one he could get away with, sort of. She knew he was being a little cheeky, but also that his statement wasn't wrong.

In the end, she made the decision, and it was to buy no headstone. When she discovered that the stones on show weren't for sale and that replicas would be made to order, it put her off. Too many people would have bought the same version, which killed exclusivity. Ultimately she'd find a bespoke designer online and do right by Sam that way.

Back in the car, Marie offered to drive because she had

fidgety hands after the experience at the funeral parlour. Fritz agreed so he could make a phone call. It was to Jim.

'I want something you'll find strange,' he told his employee. And strange it was. He wanted to know all the names of people whose deaths he might have been responsible for.

'Directly?' Jim said. 'It's three. How can you forget that? Unless you've been up to no good in secret.'

'Not just personally. Indirectly.'

'Ordered? I think it's eighteen, but I'd have to research that.'

'There are people who died because of me, though. Not just ones I put a hit on.'

Jim laughed. 'Then we're into high figures. I mean, what filters have we got? Drugs kill people. It might be impossible to know without drawing a tree chart. I hope you're not writing your autobiography. At least give me a pseudonym if so.'

'Find out about parents of dead people. Those are the names and addresses I want to know. I want to contact them. I don't care if it sounds bizarre. Just look into it.'

Fritz hung up the phone, then hung his head. What had he just done? He knew the pain of losing a child, so was he really about to contact parents whose grief he'd caused and... what, pay them? Send flowers? It was–

A car horn cut into his thoughts. He looked up to see that his vehicle was stopped, but at a green light. Waiting cars filled his wing mirror. And Marie was staring at him. 'It shows you're hurt,' she said, nice and calm. 'That's good because you've seemed a bit cyborg-like about Sam's death. That's why I'm not shouting at you. But it also seems that your brain has come loose. You can't do what you just told Jim. The cops would be all over you like never before. Don't ever let me find out you've gone begging for forgiveness to someone whose kid you killed.'

He nodded. Marie gave the car behind the finger and continued to drive.

'I wasn't going to beg them,' he said shortly. 'I just wanted to... I don't know.'

'Forget them. Sam is all that matters to us. If you want to do right by him, give him a nice present up there in heaven. And nothing beats letting him look down and see his killers being tortured to death. There's two still running free and gloating. That's your priority.'

'*You* want them dead, Marie, not Sam. It's to make you feel better.'

'This is for Sam and don't you forget it. If only so he can look down and see his mother smiling again.'

FIFTY-ONE

Newton parked and waited with the kids while Louis headed into the shopping centre. He made the mistake of jogging to Sonia's shop, which got the attention of a security guard. Which, because they were colleagues, got him recognised. He was collared on the escalator. Louis told the man he'd just quit, and have a nice life.

Sonia was serving a customer when he rushed into the store. He waited and took his place before the counter. She said, 'I expected you to come see me before you started.' Then she noticed his clothing. 'Why aren't you in uniform?'

He would not lie. But he could tread a parallel path. 'I'm not in work for the next two weeks. Listen carefully. Newton has a static caravan on a holiday park. Free swimming. Nice walks. Close to the beach. If we agree right now, and we go right now, we can have a free holiday. Completely free. All food paid for. Bucket and spade paid for.'

She had trouble digesting what he was saying. 'Right away. But work? School? I mean, how quick is right away? Tomorrow? I–'

'Right away as in tell your boss you have bellyache, and let's go.'

She shook her head. 'What? We can't just– Is tomorrow too late? I mean... packing and–'

'Not needed. He'll buy us clothing. Don't ask why, but we have to go now or we can't have the caravan. The kids are in the car outside. Anything we need to take care of can be done by phone call, or someone pops back home. This is a last-minute, one-time thing. Let's go wild and live a bit. You wanted a holiday and this is my treat to my beautiful wife. Bellyache. Go.'

He gave her a little push towards the back office, just to get her going. She went slowly, still stunned. He left the shop and hid, because her boss wouldn't buy a bellyache story if he saw her husband lurking around.

A minute later, she returned. He took her arm when she left the shop. She said, 'I couldn't say a bellyache. I said one of the kids was ill. My boss wouldn't dare have a problem with that.'

'They'll be ill from so much fun by this time tomorrow.'

'This seems mad, Louis.'

'Mad and impromptu. That's what's fun about it. Planning is for wimps.'

He almost dragged her. Now she laughed and said, 'God, this is mad. It's like we're on the run.'

To that he had no response.

FIFTY-TWO

Marie wanted dinner out, which Fritz didn't mind. It would give him something to do, although recently activity hadn't helped get his mind off Sam the way he'd hoped. Around 6pm, he took his wife to a luxurious place just outside London. It was owned by a friend, so the food was free and the manager even shifted another couple from the prime table on the back patio. They ordered and stared at a pond illuminated by floating candles.

The reason for her good mood: earlier, after the funeral, he'd approached her in their kitchen and flipped something through the air. She had caught and been awed by it. Her son's signet ring.

'This is the life, right?' Marie now said. She held up her wine glass for a toast. Fritz had water. 'This is what we worked so hard for.'

He didn't feel happy with his life at the moment. But he knew Marie was just trying to also get her mind off Sam by concentrating on the good things. 'Yes.'

'So why is it all getting you down?'

He pretended to be puzzled. 'What do you mean? I'm all good.'

'You've been winding down for a while now. Losing the fire.'

He couldn't blame Sam's death in case it set her off. 'Age, maybe. Or enjoying the good life. I can't work hard all the time.'

She sipped and eyed him in a way he didn't like. God, he hoped she wasn't about to cause a scene. It was embarrassing enough to sit here with the fattest woman in the restaurant.

'There was a time when you were the first to start moving, Ley. It didn't matter if you were in the bath, or we were having sex. If a call came, out you went to take care of business.'

Sex with her? He couldn't remember the last time. He didn't care if it never happened again. 'Age, like I said. I have people to do things for me now.'

'No, it's not just that. You haven't mellowed, you've changed. And it's not because Sam got killed. This happened way before. You don't seem that interested anymore. You have Jim now, and over the last few years you've been relying on him more and more.'

'He's my fixer. He does the hard work, and I take it easy.'

'There was a time when you spent most of the day and night out of the house. Now you're in just about every evening. I miss that man. The one who was all action.'

And he missed the slim girl who used to fuck for hours straight, and make him laugh, and who wasn't damn well insane. Fritz wasn't sure what had slowly attracted him to men, but had assumed it was something dormant that floated to the surface in later years. Maybe, though, his own wife had put him off the female of the species.

'I just do my action with a phone these days, that's all.'

The food came. Marie had ordered Scandinavian steak. He

had cottage pie. She ate one mouthful and said, 'You lost the fire.'

Jim had accused him of the very same thing just weeks ago. Fritz had laughed it off, but now he felt the urge to be honest. He had thought about this long and hard, and he knew his new persona wasn't entirely due to the loss of a son. That had only highlighted it. He decided to voice his inner feelings, even though he knew Marie would blast them like clay ducks.

'You're right, it's not just about Sam. I had something to strive for. I was building an empire. It's now built.'

She smiled, but it was all wrong. 'You have all the respect and power in the world? We have enough money? We could buy ten islands?'

That annoyed him. 'We've got enough for what we need. There's such a thing as too much. Now, I want to enjoy life.'

'You don't enjoy the power?'

'I did. But now it's a means to an end. I never had a peaceful moment. That wore on me. Now I'd like a quiet life. That's why I stay indoors a lot. Worrying all the time is no good for anyone. I'm a target. I can't even go to the shop for eggs without panicking that some lunatic is lurking in the bushes.'

She waited for more, seemingly unconvinced. 'Marie, there's thousands of people who'd love to take me down. They know my face, but I don't know theirs. And then there's the police. They're probably huddled in an office right now, scheming to lock me up. And too many people rely on me. It's all a big headache, if I'm honest.'

She laughed and shook her head. That hurt him. He had bared his soul to a woman he little cared about anymore. He wondered if he was still with her only because he didn't want to grow old alone. He had Josh, but that was a secret life and the boy was much younger. When Fritz hit sixty, Josh would only be thirty-three. He'd lose interest one day. It might even happen soon, if he got sick of being cooped up in the farmhouse 24/7.

He pictured Josh, naked, both of them having fun, and that eased the hate he felt for Marie. He still had more to unload, though. 'When you're at the top, you can only go down. The higher you are, the bigger the fall.' He leaned back in his chair, and next said something he'd dreaded telling her for months now. 'I want out.'

'Out?' she said around a mouthful of food. 'Of crime?'

He looked around to make sure none of the other diners had heard her. 'Yes. I'll be honest and say I've thought about it for a long time. Then we lost Sam and that seemed to enhance it all. It made me understand. His death was the first time in a long time that I've felt *compelled* into doing something... big and bad. It made me realise that's not me anymore. People change.'

Marie paused. A tear ran from her eye. Emotion like this from her was rarer than *T. rex* fossils, and it made him regret that he hadn't made her happier. That he hadn't somehow prevented her mind from going rotten. She would never find another man if he left her.

She pushed her half-empty plate away. 'I understand. We lost our boy. He was taken because of the life we live. If you want out, we can do that. If you want us to become couch potatoes, we can do that.'

Really? 'In a new house. Somewhere where my face isn't known. Down in a remote part of Kent or Surrey. Somewhere that still has giant marrow competitions.'

She smiled at him. 'Okay, baby, we can do that. We can do that soon. We'll get away from the crime life and go become bumpkins. We'll live in a converted barn. We'll grow giant marrows.'

Fritz smiled. He loved the idea, but only because life would

175

be less stressful if a new start fixed Marie's bent mind. 'We'll drink ale from flagons and build a scarecrow.'

She raised her glass and smiled. All of a sudden, she had a pretty face again. Was the old Marie back? He clinked his glass against hers. Just for a fleeting second, he wondered if there was a chance that, normal again, Marie might rekindle the love for her that he'd lost long ago. Might he even pick her over Josh?

Then her eyes got steely. 'As soon as we've got revenge for Sam. When the last of his killers is gutted and dead and buried, we'll go live your dream. So why don't you speed things along, stop wasting time, and do something useful to find these murdering bastards?'

Fritz glanced around the room. Myriad eyes looked right back.

PART 3

FIFTY-THREE

Havendale Resort, Cleethorpes. Five minutes from the beach and, more important to the kids, three minutes from a McDonald's. They filled their faces with drive-thru grub as Newton drove into the holiday park and spoke to the lady manning the bar at the pub, who was also the receptionist. It was just after 9pm.

They drove up the single main road, off which were side lanes with the caravans arranged along both edges. They found lane T, turned in, and stopped at plot twenty-two. It was a winterised home and had decking with a built-in hot tub.

That electrified the kids. Sonia was impressed by the living room and three bedrooms. Louis liked the giant living room TV. Newton zeroed in on a cupboard that contained spirits and lagers. He poured the adults much-needed drinks.

The kids wanted to soak in the tub, but nobody had swimming gear and they had to use their underwear. Since it was now dark, they turned off the exterior light and used the tub illuminations. The caravans either side were empty, so the area was peaceful and quiet.

The kids were determined that bedtimes didn't apply on

holiday, so Sonia agreed to take them shopping for clothing and breakfast material. Newton loaned her his car and bank card, the latter of which she was ordered not to go 'berserk' with.

'Berserk is her only gear when it's free money,' Louis said.

When she and the kids were gone, Newton showed Louis his phone. He had it set up to receive feed from six cameras dotted around and outside his house. Impressive. The house and gardens were dark and, most important, empty.

'What the hell is that?' Louis said, pointing. Newton quickly shifted from the bedroom camera to another, but too late. 'Was that a bondage mask on the shelf? Wow. Dark horse.'

'It was a gas mask.'

'They come with dildos these days?'

'Piss off. Concentrate on what matters. No bombs. No bad guys hiding behind the sofa.'

'Early days,' Louis said, and he got no argument.

Sonia was back by ten and the group went to the pub, where the kids played on a claw machine that they were certain was fixed. Sonia and Newton played pool, and she wiped him so badly he challenged her to golf one day. Louis watched the news, but saw nothing relevant.

At one point he overheard Sonia asking Newton about whether or not he wanted kids, and he saw the man's discomfort as he struggled through that conversation. Newton mentioned his long hours again. But he didn't say no, he didn't want kids.

Later still, when the kids were asleep, Sonia read a Jane Heafield book in bed and Louis and Newton drank beers on the decking. It was a cloudless night and stars were visible.

'Gave your wife that money yet?' Newton said. 'So I don't have to keep using mine.'

Louis shook his head. 'I will. When I'm not worried about all the questions.'

'Where is it? Here?'

'Yep. Behind the sofa. I'll get to it at some point.'

Newton pointed at a dot that moved across the sky. 'That could be the space station. How cool would it be to be on that? They get a sunrise every forty-five minutes or so.'

'Yeah, cool. Nobody up there is getting their heads cut off.'

He checked London news for any mention of raided homes or breaks in the Sam Fritz murder or any mention of Owen Moore. Nothing. They continued to drink.

'Good luck for the rest of the night,' Louis said. It wasn't entirely a joke.

FIFTY-FOUR

Marie had insisted that Fritz was there in person when the
doorman was captured. He agreed. When she went for a bath at
8.30pm and he brought her her half-empty bottle of wine, she
reminded him that she wanted a head for her receipts spike.
Finally, he called her bluff on that.

'Okay, maybe that's extreme,' she said, sipping her wine
straight from the bottle. 'But video it. I want proof that he
suffered.'

He was fine with both orders. He called Jim to arrange a car
to pick him up from home in an hour. He wanted Spotter on the
team, but told Jim to tell the kid nothing about the job yet.
When he went back upstairs half an hour later, he found Marie
asleep in the bedroom, the empty bottle discarded on the floor.
She'd be out all night, he knew. So he headed downstairs,
unpackaged a brand-new burner, and called Jim.

'Cancel my car. I'm staying here.'

'No problem. Sure you don't want to do the kill? You missed
out on Moore.'

He couldn't be bothered with all the hassle and didn't want

to sit in a cold car for hours. 'I'm good. Just make sure it's videoed. I'll watch that.'

'Live?'

A live kill by video call? Interesting. But he'd have to hang around and wait for a call. And if he saw gruesome torture, it might make sleep longer to come by. 'No. I'll watch it tomorrow. But send the team by so I can talk to them.'

He hung up. The car arrived shortly afterwards. This late, he didn't need to worry about his nosey neighbour, so he buzzed the car through the gates and allowed it to park right outside his house. He went out. The driver was a man he'd once been an enforcer with, years back. He was in his fifties now and beyond all that brash nonsense, but Fritz felt loyal and kept him around. They shook hands.

In the front passenger seat was a young man in trousers and a blue shirt. He was handsome and Fritz tried not to look long and hard. In the back were two vicious bastards, and sandwiched between them, and looking deathly uncomfortable, was Spotter. He'd been told only that he had a job to do and to wear his best clothing. Which was a bright white shirt, surprisingly neat and clean, and black trousers.

Fritz said to him, 'This chap in the front is your partner tonight. He's supposed to give you the instructions, but I'm going to run through it for you. You're off to Fōda. Eat what you want. You'll be there about 10pm, but the place is open late.'

'What if they don't let me in? I know I look dodgy.'

He did. Bad teeth, patchy skin. 'You'll be fine. As long as your money looks good. Now listen carefully. You'll get this repeated, but here's the plan...'

He outlined it. Restaurants didn't take payment up front. Spotter would eat, then try to run. The doorman would give chase.

'What if he doesn't?' Spotter said.

'It's his job. Run out and down an alley alongside the building. There is a recessed fire exit for the restaurant. My two friends by your side will be in that fire exit, and they'll take over. You just run and run. Got it?'

Spotter nodded. 'Yes, sir. It'll be a pleasure.'

'You haven't got anything with your ID on it, have you? Just in case you get caught.'

'No,' Spotter said. It wasn't quite a lie. Unknown to Fritz, Spotter had last worn his best trousers for an appointment, at which he'd been given something. Just after getting in the car, he'd found it in his pocket. He'd already gotten rid of it.

'Good,' Fritz said. 'Then you just run once you're out of the restaurant. Run and enjoy your money.'

Spotter nodded. He seemed calmer now. If only he'd been smarter. The kid knew the sordid details of a murder plot that could sink a top crime baron. Only an idiot would think he wouldn't be silenced to prevent that.

FIFTY-FIVE

Fritz got news of the capture while he paced in the back yard. He was too wired to sleep. Jim called at 11.16 and told him the mission had been a success. The doorman was now in the cellars beneath 25 Penistone Road. Fritz told him to wait a mo and headed indoors. He sat at the kitchen table and resumed the conversation.

'Before you tell me, Jim. Spotter. Dead yet?'

'No, we've got him held at–'

'Let him go. I've changed my mind. I like the kid.'

Jim paused. Always a good sign the man didn't agree with a decision. 'He knows too much.'

'Just remind him of the consequences of telling tales. The kid got me eggs. Leave him. Cut him loose. Now, tell me about the doorman.'

Allen Jackson was the man's name, according to his driver's licence. He seemed to have no obvious connection to Moore and wasn't ex-army. He also was claiming no knowledge of the ninja attack. 'You want to head down to Penistone and do him?' Jim asked.

'No, do video the kill, like I said.' Fritz thought. 'Think he'll talk?'

'Sure. He's not former army like Moore was. The chaps who worked on Moore were too heavy-handed. You know the romper crew is more experienced.'

'Okay. Call me when–'

'You got him?' Marie said. He turned. She was lurking just outside the kitchen doorway, her eyes droopy. So much for being asleep all night. This was the second time she'd sneaked up on him during a vital phone call.

He nodded. She held out her hand for the phone. He gave it over. She put it on speakerphone and laid it on the table. 'Has he got a family?'

Ever-professional Jim sounded uncommonly flustered. 'Marie? Er...hello. Not sure about that. Why? Ley, am I good to talk to Marie about this?'

'Don't be rude, Jim,' she snapped. 'My husband will back up what I say, don't you worry. You have the doorman's licence, which means you have an address. Go down there. Take his family, especially if there's a young child. Then he'll talk. And send a car for Ley so he can get his hands bloody. You boys really do need a woman's touch in all of this.'

She hung up the call and turned to her husband. 'Get off your lazy arse and go down there. The video is a good idea, but for me. And on it I want to see you cut that man's throat and stab his eyes out. Understand? Show some love for your dead son.'

And on that bombshell, she returned to bed.

FIFTY-SIX

'Crash the car.'

The driver, a new guy recruited by a regular, looked at Fritz in the rear-view mirror. 'Sorry, sir?'

'Actually, don't crash. Just find somewhere to park. Somewhere we won't stand out.'

The driver didn't question it. He chose a supermarket car park. It was a twenty-four hour joint, surprisingly busy at midnight, and they were lost in the crowd. Fritz played a game on his phone until he got a call. Jim. Fritz learned that the restaurant doorman's house had been visited, but nobody had been there and he seemed to live alone. No sign of his car. 'Are you nearly there?'

'Yes,' Fritz lied, and hung up. The driver read this as a sign that it was time to get on the move, so he started the engine. 'Turn it off,' Fritz told him. 'We're going to just sit here. You got any audiobooks for the stereo.'

'No, sorry.'

'Go into that store and buy one. Non-fiction if you can find it.'

The driver didn't find one, but he managed to connect

Fritz's phone to the stereo via Bluetooth, and they both listened to a story about the use of animals in World War II. About an hour later, Fritz turned it off, annoyed at his stupidity.

He thought back to his first day at senior school, which had terrified him. He woke, ate breakfast, got his schoolbag, got his packed lunch, dressed, and headed out of the house. And walked around a local shopping mall all day.

How many times had he performed that pantomime? Of going through the motions of preparing for a school day – to fool his mother – while planning to play truant? He'd been embarrassed by such immature behaviour, yet look at him now. He'd considered faking a car crash just to avoid slaying a man at the romper room.

Now he was killing time in a car park. What sneaky trick might he have performed if he'd reached Penistone Road – dressed another man in his clothing and videoed the murder from an angle that hid his face?

'Take me home,' he told the driver.

Balls to this charade. He would go back and tell Marie he didn't want to personally kill the doorman. As long as the man died, the job was done. He called Jim.

'Tell the boys to move ahead without me. I'm not coming down. Just tell them to kill the doorman and do it soon. But get it filmed. Marie wants her snuff movie!'

No sense in poking the bear. Back home, he sneaked into the house, but needn't have bothered. The bear was asleep in bed again. He sat downstairs to work on what he'd say to her in the morning.

In the end, the problem got solved for him. Jim called just minutes later with news.

'The doorman is dead. He didn't hold up. Someone tried to cut off his ear, but he struggled and... well, his throat. They tried to stop the bleeding. No good. Sorry, boss.'

He didn't sound sorry, and nor was Fritz. Another of the ninjas was gone. Mission accomplished. 'Get me a photo of him. The slashed throat is good. I'll tell the wife I did it.'

'Sure. I'll have the body disposed of. Properly, this time.'

'That would be nice.'

FIFTY-SEVEN

McDonald's. Playpark. Swimming pool. The kids were playing tag with others. Sonia and Louis were floating in a corner, just shooting the breeze. Newton was in another corner, using his phone.

Louis saw him look at his wrist: a universal sign for 'time'. A clock on the wall of the changing rooms said it was 10.53am.

Pub. Beach. Amusement arcade. The kids were busy being amazed that they'd found another fixed claw machine. It was just after two in the afternoon. Newton approached Louis with news. He had called his restaurant's manager, partly for business updates but also to see if any shady people had been around. His doorman, Allen, had last night chased a non-payer – and never returned. His phone was dead. Nobody was at his house, which was in Watford.

'This is wrong,' Newton said. 'He looks a little like me. This could be a case of mistaken identity.'

Louis found it hard to disagree.

He checked online for Watford's local news. Nothing of note. It didn't lift their spirits. On the fob were two electronic keys for the caravan, so Newton slipped one off and handed it to

Louis, who understood the unspoken plan. Louis had something to add.

They would both create an account on a social media platform. Each account would have only the other man as a friend. Every hour, they would post something simple, like a smiley face or a word about the weather. Not a message to the other, but just a post.

'I get it,' Newton said. 'If one of us doesn't post, the other knows there's a problem. That's a bit of pressure on me. I could forget.'

'You won't because you know I'll panic. If I don't post, I might be dead. I might just have given up your name to bad guys. If one of us doesn't post even once, the other runs to the police.'

Newton nodded. They chose Mastodon and created the accounts. Then the two men shook hands and Newton jogged from the arcade. When Sonia returned, Louis said, 'We'll have to walk back or get a taxi. Newton's had to pop back to London to check on something.'

Cautious words. He would not lie to his wife.

FIFTY-EIGHT

Newton made the roughly 180 mile journey south in three hours and was lucky not to get pulled by police for take-the-piss speeding. He parked outside a One Stop store a hundred metres from his destination. He posted to Mastodon for the second time since he'd left Cleethorpes. Louis immediately did the same.

Still no word from the Fōda doorman. Newton watched his employee's residential block for a few minutes. No activity that raised concerns. He drove closer and laid up in the car park. He could see Allen's first-floor living room window. The curtains were closed. Same for the bedroom. That didn't sit well in his gut. It was a grey-skied day, so the curtains hadn't been pulled against a bright sun. It suggested they'd remained shut since last night.

No more silly social media posts. He called Louis. 'I'm outside his flat. Doesn't look like anyone is in. Area looks pretty lame. I'll go knock on.'

'Be careful.'

Newton hung up. He exited his car and approached the entrance to the block, where he rang the buzzer for Allen's flat.

No answer. He rang another and said, 'Amazon delivery,' when a lady answered. He was buzzed in. When he reached Allen's floor, he stopped outside a different door but stared at Allen's. It was closed and undamaged. No one was around so he moved closer.

Before knocking, he bent down to peer through the letterbox. It showed him a hallway, but the door at the end, to the living room, was shut. No sounds came from within. Again, it seemed wrong, but it was proof of nothing. The guy could simply be out. Allen's phone could be lost or busted. Way down the list of possibles was kidnap by a gangster squad, but Newton couldn't shake a gut instinct that something was wrong.

He'd give it a while. Since he was in London, he'd pop by Louis's house, make sure everything was okay there, and then return here in a few hours. If there was no joy in contacting Allen, he'd rouse some neighbours and see what they knew.

FIFTY-NINE

There was little sun, but enough to help.

As Newton exited the housing block and walked across the car park, he caught a glint of brightness. In the hot desert of Afghanistan, light bouncing off windows and rifle scopes and other shiny metal was commonplace. He knew instantly that something had moved and angled sunlight into his eyes.

What exactly had reflected the light he didn't know. It didn't happen again. But his hackles were up. He couldn't help but imagine a rifle or binoculars being aimed at him. He walked to his car with a brisk pace, eager to get away but also careful not to let anyone watching know that he was spooked.

As he pulled out of the car park, another vehicle did the same further down the street. It could be unconnected, but Newton kept his eyes on it via the mirrors. The new vehicle, a red Audi, stayed fifty metres behind him to the corner, and it took the same left. Then the very next right.

Again, it could be innocent, so Newton needed another test. He pulled up outside a newsagent. The Audi slipped to the kerb a distance behind him. Back there were homes, not shops. The driver could live there, so Newton waited.

Nobody got out of the car. So there it was. Someone had been watching Allen's flat, waiting to see who showed up.

Newton climbed out of his car and approached the boot. He pretended to fiddle with it, as if there was a fault. He was driving again seconds later. And the Audi followed.

On the next street, he stopped in the middle of the road to give his boot another analysis. The driver behind him dabbed his horn. Newton gave an apology and got back behind the wheel. The Audi was three cars back, but the sole man inside had surely seen Newton messing with the boot.

Which meant his stalker wasn't suspicious when, at a red light, the target once again emerged from his vehicle and approached the boot. Newton had waited until no innocent cars were between them. He opened the boot, watched from just ten feet away by the man following him.

In a flash, he'd grabbed his heavy metal scissor jack, turned, and lobbed it. The item crashed into the Audi's windscreen, turning it into an opaque jigsaw. He then rushed to the driver's door and hauled it open. The man inside was middle-aged, thin, with ginger hair and a silly moustache. He cowered from Newton.

On the passenger seat were binoculars, which had surely caused the glint Newton had seen. There was also a mobile phone, which Newton reached across the terrified man to grab. As he did so, his free arm pressed into the man's throat to prevent an attack. Phone collected, he ran to his car and blasted through the red light. The Audi didn't follow.

SIXTY

Newton waited until he was driving again before checking the phone he'd stolen from the man following him. Luckily, it wasn't password-protected. When he flicked the screen to open it up, he almost crashed his Merc into a van heading down the opposite lane. He had to pull into the side of the road to fully digest what he was looking at.

A sent text message. It was the only sent or received message in the device and was to a number stored under no name. It said BLACK MAN AT DOORMAN PLACE and contained his Merc's registration number. Jesus hell Christ.

He called Louis, who sounded like he was in a busy food joint. 'They've got my employee for sure. Get somewhere where we can talk.'

He heard the noise of diners fade as Louis rushed to a quiet spot. 'What's happened, Newton? How do you know?'

Newton told him about the quiet flat, the closed curtains, and the tail who'd sent someone his registration. Louis cursed. 'Get out of there, Newton. Get back here, but make sure no one follows you. Your staff know you have a caravan?'

'Yeah, but nobody has been spoken to except my doorman.

And he doesn't know where it is. We don't even know if he told them anything.'

'We can't assume they don't know everything. Just get back here and let's work on our next move.'

Newton gave a tense sigh. He pulled into traffic and drove fast. 'I'll do a Mastodon post every fifteen minutes, Louis. I know my next move already. My car is still registered at my ex-wife's address.'

'Warn her or something. But you need to stay away from—'

'I've got a kid, Louis.'

This news didn't cause the shock it should have. Louis had already suspected something amiss regarding Newton and children, although he'd wondered if his old friend might have tried and failed to have one. 'I knew something was bothering you. Boy or girl?'

'Boy. He's ten. I barely see him, Louis. His mother got custody because of my long hours. I was embarrassed, mate, especially after I learned about your happy family. That's why I didn't tell you. I didn't think we'd stay connected, so lying wouldn't hurt. You've got a loving family and you're a great dad. I'm a bullshit dad who put work first.'

'No, Newton, don't say things like—'

'It's irrelevant now. All that matters is I've got a boy and he lives at that address. That's where these fuckers are going. So that's where I'm going.'

SIXTY-ONE

Marie: 'Dave's going to freak out when he learns about her new boyfriend.'

Fritz: 'Yeah.'

Marie: 'Cos Dave's got that allergy and the boyfriend has got all those dogs.'

Fritz: 'Yeah. Amazing.'

Marie: 'You think Dave will continue to chase her or go back to Lianne?'

Fritz: 'Wow. That's a puzzle.'

Some horseshit new romcom was at the cinema, and Marie wanted to see it, so there they were. He liked free time, but a more enjoyable movie would have sweetened it. Fritz wanted to keep his wife happy, so he laughed when she did, forced himself to follow the daft plot, and tried not to be annoyed that her meaty limb hogged the armrest. A few minutes later, a brand-new burner buzzed in his pocket.

'I need the toilet,' he said. 'Tell me what I miss.'

'Be quick. I reckon Dave is going to...'

He zoned her out and fled the auditorium. In a toilet cubicle, he returned a missed call from Jim. Even though he knew this was news and it might be good, he was a little peeved at the interruption to his free time.

The underboss said, 'A Black guy just went to the doorman's place. We got a car registration. I've traced it to a man called Newton Meecham. I looked online at Fōda, and he's the damn owner.'

Fritz sighed. 'We got the wrong guy. You know this Meecham's address?'

'Sure do. Headstone North, in Harrow. Apparently the happiest place in London, is Harrow.'

'Not for long. You got a plan?'

Jim sure did. It was a gimmick done to death in a thousand movies, but still one of his favourites. They had a stolen BT Openreach van. Google Earth had showed Jim a BT junction box close to the house. How fateful was that?

The van would park near the home, full of chaps in the correct uniform. One would fiddle around with the junction box, just to give everything the sincere feel. When Newton arrived, the men would swarm, detain, transport.

'After his interrogation, would you like this kill? I get the feeling you're losing interest in the personal touch. Perhaps just video of the event again?'

Fritz thought...

SIXTY-TWO

At his doorman's place, Newton had parked a safe distance away back and watched for enemies. He couldn't risk such countermeasures here. Killers could be en route right now.

He made a Mastodon post as he drove. On his ex-wife's street, he parked right across the road from his former home, between a pair of cars against the kerb. Outside her neighbour's home was a car with its hood up. A man had his head in the engine bay, fiddling. Newton pretended to watch, but his eyes were on a vehicle ten metres further down the road.

As he'd passed the works van, he'd spotted three guys sitting in the front. It faced away from him, so he could now see only the driver in the wing mirror. Were they innocent workers on a break? Or was this the kill team and they were waiting for a quiet moment to strike the house?

Only one way to find out. When he left his car, Newton gave a sly glance at the van. The driver was now watching him in the wing mirror – but was that just curiosity about the new arrival on the street? They were after a Black man, but around here the racial mix was fairly even. Maybe they were waiting for someone to approach the house.

The house itself seemed inert. In fact, he saw a shape – his ex-wife – walk past the living room window, sipping from a cup. She didn't appear to be the captive of monsters. He relaxed a little.

However, she wasn't safe yet and the van was still a worry. He couldn't approach his former home without giving away his identity. Then he had an idea.

Newton didn't know the guy who lived next door, but he wanted to do the neighbourly thing and help him fix his car. It might convince the men in the van that this Black guy wasn't the one they wanted.

Still wary of the van but hiding his scrutiny, he went to his boot and got jump cables.

He yelled out, 'Hey, pal. Need any help? I was just passing. Thought I'd do the good Samaritan thing. Lucky for you, last night I watched that movie, *Pay it Forward*.' He showed off the cables, hoping the goons would spot them.

The man fixing the car looked up and said, 'Hey, that'd be great, mate. I'm on a schedule. Cheers.'

Perfect. The goons would believe he was just helping out a fellow human. They wouldn't think twice if Newton then went round back of the neighbour's home – perhaps to fetch a tool. There, out of sight, he could leap the fence and get to his ex-wife's back door. He'd then get her out, and together they'd go fetch Bart from school. Hopefully, if things went well, his boy would be playing with Louis's kids in a couple of hours.

The problem was getting to the car and away, but he wasn't thinking that far ahead. Bizarrely, right then he was more worried about the awkward chat he was about to have with his ex-wife.

SIXTY-THREE

...and then Fritz said, 'Actually, get the leader of whatever team you're using to call me.'

Jim paused. 'Call you? Why?'

'Just do that, please.'

Jim agreed, but he obviously didn't like even the big boss messing with his fine-tuned schemes. Fritz waited in the sweetly quiet toilet cubicle and the call came within two minutes. The new guy introduced himself as Larry.

Fritz said, 'Change of plan. Forget anything to do with video cameras. And you won't be kidnapping anyone, so lose your team. Wherever it's going down, I want you and you alone to kill Newton Meecham. Understand?'

Larry said he did, but he mentioned Jim. Jim had been quite specific about his plan being carried out to the letter.

'When Jim becomes king, you can do what he says. Is he king?'

'No, sir.'

'Who is?'

'You, sir.'

'So let's have no more dangerous backchat. You, alone, right now. No silly phone company trick. Take a stolen car. Pretend the car is busted. Have a hand under the bonnet. Have a knife in that hand. When Meecham is in range, kill him quick.'

Fritz almost heard Larry gulp. 'In the street, sir?'

'In the street. Make sure he's dead, or I'll be sending you a doctor's coat so you can finish the job down at the ICU ward. We're still looking for one more man, so give the body a quick search. After that, go with whatever Jim set up for alibiing you and getting rid of the vehicle. Don't hurt anyone who might be with Meecham.'

Fritz hung up. He was tempted to sit a while longer and enjoy the quiet. Strangely, though, he wanted to know what Romcom Dave would do next.

SIXTY-FOUR

Louis told Sonia he still had Newton's debit card, which was true, but he chose to use cash from the envelope containing ten grand to buy his family a hearty evening meal at a pub restaurant with a games room for kids. Louise and Theo were over the moon, but Sonia wasn't. Louis was scared and he knew his wife could sense something amiss with him.

He tried to hide it, but his mood darkened with each passing fifteen minutes that delivered no word from Newton. It was now past 8pm and his friend still hadn't posted to Mastodon.

The kids were busy and Sonia said, 'I'm going to get another wine. Another beer for you?'

He shook his head. She headed to the bar and Louis pulled out his mobile. He typed Newton's number in, then paused with his finger over the call button. If his friend had been captured, they had his phone. The number wasn't stored in the device, but that didn't mean anything. Not if Newton had been forced to give it up.

Knowing they could trace the device, he broke his mobile apart, including the sim card. They were safe here for now, so he tried to put on a game face when Sonia returned.

'You okay?' she said. 'Deadly quiet this evening. Newton okay?'

'He won't be back tonight,' he said. They were carefully chosen words

She sipped and eyed him. 'Something's wrong, Louis. I can read you. Something I should know about? Something to do with this impromptu holiday?'

'Listen, why don't you go the lounge to have that wine? Have another. Because we have a problem. I lost Newton's bank card somewhere. I need to get the other one from his room at the caravan. Unless you want to wash pots with me?'

She looked horrified. 'Lost it? Where?'

They had walked to the restaurant, just a half mile down the road, by using the beach. That was where he'd lost the card, he said. It was still in his coat pocket, right alongside the thick envelope of cash. The lie burned his innards. It was the first time he'd bullshitted his wife. 'It'll be floating out to sea by now. Be funny if a castaway found it.'

'That's not funny, Louis. We owe for the meal.'

'I know. That's why I'll go back to the caravan. You wait here with the kids. They're having fun. Use the lounge. Add another wine to the table order. I'll be an hour, tops.'

Still the suspicious eyes, but she questioned him no further. She knew he would never lie to her. But he had. If there was anything that proved he now believed something terrible had happened to Newton, it was that. There was no doubt now that he was the last man standing.

He left the restaurant and, once out of sight, started running. Along the way, he dumped the pieces of his phone. He got to the holiday park in eight minutes. The entrance gates never shut, so he walked in. It was dark, but holidaymakers were everywhere.

The show bar had an event on and people mingled outside.

205

Nearby was the playpark and tennis court, from which emerged the noise of kids playing. He was confident he could walk to the caravan without issue and set off down the road.

He was wary of everyone and everything. A couple walked past him, and he turned to make sure they ignored him. They did. A man paced him on the opposite side of the road, so Louis slowed down to let him get ahead. The man didn't look round. A red car came towards him. And cruised past. The low speed was unnerving, but the speed limit was ten. A black car came from behind. And cruised past.

SIXTY-FIVE

'Newton Meecham is dead. Anti-climactic, no? A case of tell, not show. I'm truly surprised you wanted no part. But he's not dead and buried. He's dead in the middle of a street. Police everywhere. Was that a wise move? I would say no.'

Fritz listened with only half an ear as Jim moaned about the method his boss had employed to wipe out Newton. He was lounging in his dark back yard, but he'd dragged his chair to the far end so he couldn't hear his wife. Marie had so enjoyed the romcom that she was in a good mood and singing loudly in the kitchen while cleaning. But now Jim's constant whine was disturbing the peace.

'Be quiet, Jim. I'm the boss. I made an executive decision. I wanted the man dead and he is.'

'By coincidence there was a legitimate team of men in a works van at the scene. And nobody thought them suspicious. It proves my plan would have worked, and we would have gotten Meecham's body. But now the police have it. Very soon they'll know Meecham was an army colleague of Moore's. They'll find the others who served. Guy number three is probably in hiding and the authorities will soon realise he's missing. And when they work out that all these men are tied to your son's murder, you'll be in deep trouble.'

'I'm always being tied to something. They can prove nothing, as always. It's your job to make sure of that, so do some making sure. Now, have you got anything approximating good news?'

Jim got over his butt being hurt nice and quick. 'The man you sent to kill Meecham found a key on him. The fob said it's from Havendale Holiday Park, up in Cleethorpes. A key for a caravan. I don't think our targets decided they needed a holiday. They ran. It's obvious they know we're onto them. Meecham obviously returned, but I reckon our third man is still down there. I already sent some men since it's two hours away. Was that okay?'

Fritz felt a sudden lightness in his gut. It felt like arriving home after the workday from hell, and he knew what it meant. He could see the end. One more guy to finish, and it would be all over. Sam would be avenged. Fritz could move on with his plans to get out of this game and start a new, more peaceful life.

'Sure, Jim. Well done.'

'Since you've lost the desire to personally kill these men, and because there's only one enemy remaining, can I assume this is to be a simple mission? In and out? No bells and whistles?'

'No bells and whistles, Jim. Do whatever damage control you need afterwards, but kill the man where he's found.'

'Video?'

'Is that a bell or a whistle?'

SIXTY-SIX

The black car, a Honda CR-V, kept Louis's attention until it passed by lane T and took the next right, onto U. He paused at the edge of T, peering down, looking for an anomaly in the vicinity of his caravan. All was still, silent, empty.

He walked down the lane. As he drew alongside the end of his caravan and stepped onto the grass, he spotted men. Three of them on the grass between lanes T and U, walking in his direction. Behind them, visible between two homes, the Honda was parked on U, facing the exit. A fourth man sat behind the wheel. The engine idled, but the lights were off.

Louis veered to retake the tarmac and moved on, to give the impression he was headed for a caravan further down the lane. He knew he could get away with a quick glance, as anyone would do out of curiosity if they heard people nearby. The three men, all the sort nobody would willingly mess with, saw him look. But they, too, knew a passerby might turn his head if he caught peripheral movement. He minded his business after that, and they did the same.

Their business was definitely him. Somehow they'd found him. Owen was dead, a guy with no connection to this lark had been killed, and now it sure looked like Newton had also fallen foul of these vicious bastards. But there was no time for sorrow, or even fear or anger. As he turned to walk towards T5, he saw the trio of men circle his caravan, trying to look in the windows.

Once out of sight alongside T4, he increased speed. He darted past the caravan and across ten metres of open space, towards a mobile home on lane U. He slid down its flank and exposed a single eye past the end. The Honda was five metres away, its rear to him. The driver had his head turned left, to stare out the passenger window and watch his colleagues in action.

There was a loud bang from the direction of Louis's caravan. The door giving way under a boot. Louis stepped into the lane and crept towards the Honda, praying the driver wouldn't look in his mirrors.

The driver's window was down. The driver was still looking the other way, oblivious to the threat from the man he was here to hurt. Louis stood tall once at the door, and threw his hands inside. Chokes were the only good offence in Louis's armoury, but for the fourth time he snapped one into place before his enemy could react.

The driver was also restrained by his seatbelt, so he had only hands with which to mount a defence. First, they threw punches past his own head, to target Louis's, but in his panic the blows hit the roof of the car. He then clawed at the forearm across his throat, and the hand on the back of his head. The endeavour was just as useless.

As the man's vigour weakened, Louis stared out the far window, and through the one in the back of his caravan. He could see the other three men ransacking the place, probably looking for clues as to where their target had gone.

Thirteen seconds after the choke was applied, Louis released it. The driver slumped forward, unconscious. Louis opened the door, released the seatbelt, and dragged him out. As he thumped to the ground, one leg fell under the car. Louis didn't care.

He got behind the wheel and slammed the door. Across the way, one of the men framed in the caravan's large back window did a double-take at the glass. He yelled something. All three men vanished from the frame and burst through the door. Two climbed the decking rail and raced across the grass, but the third chose a different tactic and used the steps to reach lane T.

Louis threw the car in gear. The Honda bumped as the offside rear wheel lurched over the sleeping man's leg. He turned the corner, onto the main drag, and stamped on the accelerator. The two bozos who'd come straight at him were left behind, but not the cleverer third. As the Honda blew past lane T, that man was there to greet him. He grabbed at the passenger door and managed to open it, then the handle was ripped from his fingers.

A moment later, all three men were in Louis's rear-view mirror.

The passenger door was wide open. Louis couldn't reach it without getting out of his seat, which would mean stopping. No chance. As he blasted through the open gateway to leave the park, he veered slightly left. A brick gatepost lowered the Honda's resale price, but it shut the door.

SIXTY-SEVEN

Some years ago, a man called Alfie Townsend left a pub on Forest Road in Waltham Forest, saw a fellow human walking ahead, and decided he wanted that man's gear. The road ran east-west between three bodies of water at Walthamstow Reservoirs and was quiet at that time of night.

Alfie followed the stranger all the way across, then pulled his jumper up over his face, covered his head with the hood of his coat, and attacked as the man was passing a gateway onto a path that ran alongside Low Maynard reservoir. Alfie dragged the man down the path and robbed him. For good measure, Alfie stripped the guy and lobbed him and his clothing into the water.

The victim had happily handed over his watch, for it had a powerful tracker that would allow him to find the thief. He made a call when he got to a phone box, wearing his sodden clothing. His name was Jim, and his call was to Fritz. Soon the tracker gave up an address.

The next evening, three hard cases in masks invaded a house and found three residents in the living room: a middle-aged man and his elderly mum and dad. Aghast, the parents watched as their son was dragged away. He was driven to the very spot Jim had been mugged, and here he got a sledgehammer to the lower spine and the elbows.

He was stripped and held until Jim had answered a video call, so he could watch the thief get thrown naked into the water. But on the screen Jim saw a face he didn't recognise.

The victim turned out to be Andy Townsend, father to Alfie. The kidnappers had assumed the younger man in the house was their target, without enquiring as to who else might be present. Alfie had been upstairs in his bedroom at the time of the attack, actually playing on the stolen phone. Andy's claims of innocence, of knowing nothing about a mugging, had been sincere.

Oh dear. The kidnappers took Andy to the nearest hospital and dumped him outside. There was a thief still unrepentant, though, so they immediately returned to the house. Police were in attendance by now, so it was a waiting game.

Mere minutes after the officers had left with useless statements, in went three men and out came four. At the reservoir, Alfie got the sledgehammer to his hips and shoulders, making movement impossible. Like swimming.

The father, Andy, still lived with his parents and now used a wheelchair because his legs wouldn't work. He'd learned to live with his grief, but all the old horror came flooding back when a trio of men simply walked into his house and demanded that he accompany them.

His chair was lifted and placed into the back of a van, which then drove to Forest Road, and here he was removed and wheeled down the same old path, where a man stood with a backpack. The location, and recognising the man who awaited him, sent his brain into a kind of shock. He was whispering Bible verses as his chair was brought to a stop in front of the man.

'I lost my kid,' Fritz said. Andy looked at him, but didn't seem quite there. No matter. Fritz didn't need a two-way conversation. 'I brought you here to show you that this is no trick. I could have killed you easily. But my people will take you home after this. I'm here just to apologise. You're the one I regret the most. You lost your boy because of me. I lost mine because of me, too.'

Fritz put the satchel on the paraplegic's legs and opened it. It was full of paper money. Still the man in the wheelchair seemed zombified. Maybe it wasn't fear, but a remnant of his son's murder years back. Fritz said nothing further and walked away.

.

SIXTY-EIGHT

Louis gave Sonia it in pieces. And in stages she fell to pieces.

A restaurant was no scene for his wife to learn that their family was in danger and her husband would, at best, serve a life sentence for murder. He collected Sonia and the kids and drove them to a hotel. He got a room using Newton's bank card and thankfully didn't need to show identification.

As soon as she'd seen the car, and the damaged passenger door, she'd known something was badly wrong, but for the kids' sake she said nothing until the youngsters were in another new bed. She dragged Louis into their bedroom.

'You stole that car. We ran from our home. And I now know that *ran* is the right word. No Secrets Hour, Louis. Tell me what's wrong.'

'That night, last Saturday, when we...'

He couldn't find the words. She offered them. 'Someone got badly hurt.'

'Owen killed a man,' he said immediately. He saw her become a little unstable inside, but she waited for more.

He was the son of a major crimelord called Ley Fritz. Now he's after us. He killed Owen. That's why we ran.

Major structural components crumbled.

He killed one of Newton's employees, which is why he went back to London.

Foundations faltered, but held.

Now Newton is missing and I think he's dead. When I went back to the caravan, it was to check to see if everything was okay. Some men were there. I barely escaped. They know where we are. We can't go back there, and we can't go home.

Full collapse.

She took her time to recover. At first, she demanded solitude, but begged him to stay before he'd reached the door. She didn't want to be touched, but soon they held each other. She called him stupid, bad, a liar, a rotten father, but she apologised for all of it.

He got her a whiskey from the mini bar, then more. It helped. She accessed the internet on her phone to find out all she could about the man who'd ruined her life.

Afterwards, she slapped her own face, but not in anger. It was the kind of move a sportsman might make to get himself in gear. She went to the window and stared out. 'We have to go to the police.'

'Sonia, this man–'

'Shut your mouth. Based on recent events, right now no idea you have is worth anything. Do you think I'm going to drag my children around hotels until they're old enough to run for their own lives? We're going to the police. Witness protection, new identities, something like that, I don't know. It all sounds wild, I know. But then this whole thing is a bizarre nightmare.'

'You're right. The police is probably the best way.'

'But not tonight. Not this late. I want our kids to sleep. Unfortunately, they can't right now.'

'Why?'

'If this man, Fritz, is everything the media claims, then he'll have means and ways. He found you fools, and he found the caravan. Maybe he can trace where bank cards are used. And you just used a dead man's to get this room.'

She was right. They woke the children and hustled them out. They drove into Grimsby, where they found a bedsit with secluded rear parking, so they could hide the stolen vehicle. Sonia picked it and it wasn't lost on Louis that a police station was barely a hundred metres down the road. He checked in alone at the desk while Sonia hung back, and he used cash she'd given him. The ten thousand pounds in the envelope was still untouched.

Despite the late hour and the husk that Sonia had become, the owner asked no questions. Once in their room, Sonia and Louis did their best to act as if everything was hunky around their kids.

Lying in bed, little Louise said, 'Will I wake somewhere else again?'

That started Sonia's tears again. She said, 'No, because your mother is in charge now.'

The eight-year-old missed the hidden message. Louis didn't.

Finally, past midnight, two little ones entered dreamland. Sonia grabbed Louis's arm and pulled him to his feet. 'Go get rid of that car. Far away. Fritz might be able to access ANPR and trace it here. We'll walk to the police station in the morning.'

He wouldn't ever doubt her fortitude. She'd just had a tonne of life-changing news dumped on her, but had remained sharp and logical. He'd had the same news piecemeal, over time, and hadn't coped half as well as she had. So he got his damn shoes on.

'Search the car,' she added. 'There might be something important that can help the police.'

She lay down as he headed for the door. He heard her begin to sob as he shut it behind him.

PART 4

SIXTY-NINE

Fritz was an idiot. Tranquillity, even at 10pm? Uninterrupted evening in the back yard with an audiobook and a shot of whiskey? Don't be a fool.

He answered his phone with a fake, long sigh. Childish? He didn't care. His next sigh was real, as Jim imparted the news from Cleethorpes. The men sent to wipe out the last of his son's killers had failed.

'Did you recruit toddlers from nursery?'

It got worse. The man had escaped by taking the vehicle the men drove up in.

Fritz said, 'Can we tell the police that the car we stole has been stolen?'

'We still don't have a name for this man. There was nothing in the caravan.'

Ever-robotic Jim was uncommonly angry. To his own surprise, Fritz wasn't. Or was that a surprise? Two of his son's three killers were now dead, yet still he felt empty. He doubted he'd cartwheel when the sole remaining fugitive also fell.

Failure was all about power and ego, and that shit didn't mean as much to him these days. Did he have to *personally* send his son's killers to their graves? Would his pride as a tough gangster suffer if the man's downfall came at someone else's hands?

No, it wouldn't. So: 'Call the cops in. Moore, Meecham, and their faceless friend. Tell them that, and let them hunt a ghost. And tell them why these men killed my boy. Newspapers would love to put the word *ninjas* in a headline.'

Another of those goddamn annoying pauses from Jim. This time he had no patience for it. 'Just do what I say. The ghost is running around the country. That playground is too big. Let the cops shrink his world to a prison cell. Much easier for us to get to him then-'

Jim abruptly hung up. Fritz stared at his phone in disbelief. Second-guessing the boss was one thing, but this was a whole new level of insolence. Jim seemed to have forgotten who was in charge.

On that thought, Fritz headed to the security office. One guard was asleep on the bunk bed, while the other watched the security monitors. That man sat up straight when Fritz burst in. 'Any attackers out there dressed as bushes?'

The security guard actually glanced at the monitors, as if he might have missed such a thing. 'All quiet, sir.'

'As always. Nobody has ever stormed this place. So I don't need you guys. Get your pal up and clear out. I'll find some other jobs for you. Get you into the field, get you some action. Go now, please. But don't wake my wife.'

She was asleep in bed, where she seemed to be spending more and more time, but he didn't trust she'd stay there. After the two men had gotten their stuff and crept out, he went back into the rear yard to make a call. He did it while staring at the back door, determined that she'd never again creep up on him.

Detective Sergeant Manning answered on the third ring. 'You're free, Manning. I'm cutting you loose.'

The detective was highly suspicious and almost in tears. 'No, you're going to kill me. You'll tell the police about me. Please. I've been loyal to you.'

Once upon a time, Fritz would have enjoyed seeing a man plead for leniency. Now it disgusted him. 'Stop whining. It's no trick, Manning. The evidence I have against you? I'll burn it. I promise. You're not accusing me of being a man who breaks his word, are you?'

'No, no, sir, I wouldn't ever.'

'Well, there's my word on a silver platter. The pictures, the audio, everything I've got against you. Up in smoke. You're free. There's no gold watch, but thanks for your service. But do me a favour, okay?'

Manning's pause said that, again, he was full of mistrust. 'Of course. Anything.'

'From now on, stay away from underaged girls.'

SEVENTY

Around midnight, Fritz made sure Marie was still asleep, then grabbed his car keys. While driving, he made a call. He used his main phone, which was only for legitimate contacts. That spoke volumes about his state of mind, since the man in question was far from law-abiding.

The call was to a place called The Majestic, a lap-dancing club in Clapham Junction. He got reception and could hear thudding music. He told the lady there he wanted to speak to Zander. Apparently, she knew of no Zander.

He believed her. Men like himself, and like Zander, had buffers. 'I want you to mention a few words to your superior. He'll mention those words to his boss, and so on. Soon those words will reach Zander. Those words are: Fritz, meet, now, Majestic.'

He hung up. Two miles out from Clapham Junction, he got a call on the same phone. A man, but not Zander. The man said, 'I understand a Mr Fritz wants to hire a table at our club tonight?'

Fritz laughed. 'Are you going to give me a codeword next?

Just tell Zander I'm coming. I'm on my own. Sounds mysterious and dangerous, right?'

He hung up. There was a heaving queue of mostly men outside the club. Fritz stopped his car alongside, where parking was a big no-no, and got out. As well as the bouncers, there were seven or eight more severe-looking men scattered about. On the pavements, in doorways, in cars. They looked like they were preparing to defend against an assault.

Fritz waved at one. 'Go park this somewhere. And clean the headlights.'

He aimed for the doorway. A bouncer let him straight through, to the objection of a number of those queueing. Another man, in a grey shirt and trousers, took over and escorted Fritz across the main floor, where patrons sat around tables near podiums bearing half-naked dancing girls. More girls circled the room, looking for paying company.

A lady came to Fritz's side, but he ignored her. Many of the patrons looked his way. The fact that he wore jeans – against the dress code – told them he was important. Upstairs, he was led to a private area that was nothing more than a corner roped off. A suited Indian man of about sixty sat on a sofa. Standing by his side were three white heavies in black. Fritz stepped over the velvet rope before his escort could detach it.

'Nice place. Old Victorian theatre, right? I see you've kept the performance ambience with the lap dancers.'

The escort leaned close to whisper to his boss. Zander nodded. The man departed.

Fritz said, 'This sort of set-up has been done to death on TV, Zander. An organised crime boss sitting in his own nightclub, all straight and sober.'

Zander crossed his legs. 'It seems you really did come alone to my castle. That's a risk.'

Fritz smiled. 'Castle. A good term. We are kings, in a sense.

But it's not as if we're at war. You run parts of London. I run parts of London. It's like Monopoly. Do people say, Let's go to war at Monopoly? No, they play. This is a game.'

Zander looked confused by the whole scene, and by Fritz's nonchalant demeanour. He sat forward, disarmed somewhat, and said, 'What's going on here, Fritz?'

'The game. I'm getting out of it. Knocking over my king. Taking my ball and going home.'

Zander grinned. 'You plan to go straight? It seems I'm not the only one who's been watching TV.'

'No joke. I'm disbanding the firm. I'm going to cut loose everyone who works for me. I'm going to give up everything I control. Drug routes, brothels, safe houses. All the scams, frauds, protection rackets. Every cop and politician under my thumb. I'm walking away from it all. In terms of boxing, I'm vacating the belt. Now the championship reverts to the number one contender. You.'

Zander paused, still one-part puzzled to five-parts guarded. 'And what happens to your pieces of the pie?'

'Another good term. I'll get my man to hand over names, addresses, everything. Move your men in. Eat all the pie, Zander.'

Zander sat back. 'If this is some kind of trick, Fritz...'

'I came alone. In my personal car, with its registration that is attached to my home. I'm not going straight, Zander. I'm just going. Every legitimate business I have will be sold. Everything illegal goes to you.'

'Let's say I believe you. Why would you give everything to me? You must want something in exchange.'

'Make me old.'

Zander gave a little laugh and a shake of the head. 'I knew there was a catch. How on earth do I do that?'

'By doing zilch. Or maybe a spot of damage control if I need it. I'm retiring to the country, Zander. I want to die at a hundred, happy. I don't want you as an enemy. I'm sick of looking over my shoulder. I'm sick of wondering if I'll be woken by intruders in the night. I'm sick of burner mobiles and swapping vehicles and bodyguards. Forget about me.'

'Is this because you lost your son? Very bad. A step too far in our business.'

True, but that wasn't a concrete rule and they'd both broken it in the past. Fritz put a slip of paper on the sofa. 'This is my man's mobile. Get your man to call him and arrange everything.' He stood. 'I'm going now. It would be very easy for your men to stop me. You could disappear me in a blink. I'd rather you allowed me to make myself vanish. Enjoy your new empire.'

He walked away. He hadn't lied to Zander about the distress of constantly looking over one's shoulder. He didn't want to go to bed worrying, so he headed to the toilet, which gave his enemies a real sweet opportunity to do something. They did nothing. He got to the exit and stood outside, where he could have easily been downed by a bullet. No bullet.

His car was brought around and he got in. He drove slowly, so any vehicle following wouldn't have a rough time. He found gloom under a large arched bridge, perfect for a takedown, and here he paused with his doors unlocked. No takedown.

He drove home, and he ordered the gate guard to leave the entrance wide open for half an hour, so that attackers didn't have to hop the fence. He entered his home, left the front door unlocked, turned off the alarm, and sat in the darkened living room with a desk lamp pointed at his face, so intruders wouldn't have to play hide-and-seek. No intruders. Except for Sam in vision-form and re-enacting precious memories in Fritz's mind.

Soon afterwards, he got ready for bed. While brushing his teeth, he noted his face in the mirror. He looked tired, edgy. It had been a long day. And he'd risked his life by meeting with his main rival.

He stopped. Stared at his reflection. No, his time in Zander's lair wasn't the cause of his frazzled features and unsettled stomach. The loss of his son, Sam? No. A sense of weakness at his failure to kill the final member of the gang responsible for his boy's murder? Also no.

But the ghost *was* the cause. Fritz had killed the man's friends, and alerted him to the fact that he was the next target. Fritz had acquired a new, faceless, possibly dangerous enemy, and for a man who sought calm in his world, that might prove to be a crazy mistake.

SEVENTY-ONE

Louis drove to a twenty-four-hour Asda in Alexandra Retail Park and bought a quartet of mobile phones using Newton's card. Once they were topped up, he looked for a quiet spot. This late, the car park was mostly empty, although a group of young men and women were congregated with their cars in a corner. He chose the opposite one and searched the Honda.

He'd picked the retail park because it was next door to a place called Stern Charter, which, since it was a business dealing in fishing excursions, sat at the edge of the River Freshney. A chain-link fence separated the two properties, giving him a view of fishing vessels floating in the dock and stored on the land.

Beyond a gate in the fence was a strip of tarmac running right to the water's edge. Perfect. When his search was over, he would aim the Honda at the gate, smash through, and leap out while the vehicle was still moving. The river would erase any fingerprints or DNA he'd left in the car.

The search took little time. The Honda's interior was pristine. He found only a box of vinyl gloves in – ironically – the glove box. Maybe the bad guys had stolen a clean-freak's vehicle, or they'd kept it spotless in case the police got it.

But he did find something on the back seat. A many-times folded little piece of paper was lodged in the recess for the middle seat belt buckle. He opened it up. It was a white repeat order prescription form for a male called Bruce Spence. Whatever his ailment, Spence took Lansoprazole for it. There was an address in Ickenham. Bingo. Ickenham was the location of Parry Estate.

Louis felt a stirring in his belly. Until a few seconds ago, an opaque idea had been floating deep in his mind, but it had never really rendered itself as a possibility. Now, with a name and address, he had a real stepping stone on the path towards it.

Towards confronting the key to everything: Ley Fritz.

No. He punched the driver's seat, angry with himself. Who was he kidding? History wrote him as a tough Navy Commando who'd ended lives in Operation Veritas, but he wasn't that man anymore. He was middle-aged, out to pasture, and he would be going up against innumerable foes from a lethal organised crime group. He should tie a weight and let the idea sink again into the depths.

He couldn't. The stirring in his gut remained. It wasn't eagerness for action. It wasn't a self-righteous desire to battle tyranny. It was because of his kids, and his wife. A simple father's instinct to protect. He just didn't trust that the police could do that job. Fritz was too powerful and probably had officers amongst his army.

Army. That word hung in his mind. He had the name and address of a man, and he could deal with a single man. He'd proved that, pasture or not. If that man led him to another, well, again that would be a single foe to face. The chain could lead him all the way to the top, to Fritz. Fritz commanded many, but ultimately he was not superhuman or a god. He was one man.

The notion was insane, dangerous, wild, but he couldn't dispel that buzz in his gut. In fact, it got worse. However slight, however dangerous, a chance was a chance. He got behind the wheel. But he didn't aim the Honda at the fence. He turned the nose towards the exit.

He had Sonia's mobile number in his memory and used one of his new phones to compose a message. Afterwards, he broke the device apart and lobbed the pieces out the window.

> Go to the police in the morning. Good luck with it and I'm sorry. I won't be with you. I have something to take care of first. I'll be okay, I promise. I love you and please tell Theo and Louise the same. Look under the bed.

SEVENTY-TWO

'What the hell are you playing at?'

The ringing phone had woken Fritz. It was barely eight in the morning. He took the call, but decided he was in no mood for Jim's crap and threw the phone to the bottom edge of the bed.

But his underboss was so enraged that Fritz still heard his voice. He sat up and grabbed the Samsung before it woke Marie. Naked, he left the room, shut the door behind him, and took the call in the upstairs hallway.

'I just got a call from one of Zander Bajaj's people,' Jim said. 'I think you know what it's about.'

'Sure do. Zander is taking over all the crap that interests the police. Maybe they'll leave me alone.'

'You can't do this, Ley. Just give away all our assets. It's unheard of. If Zander controls…'

Fritz covered the speaker while Jim responded. He heard only a faint buzz, but he knew his second-in-command would be ranting about Zander's new power and his elevated danger to Fritz's firm and all that malarky.

When the noise ceased, which meant Jim had stopped

rabbiting, Fritz said, 'You're right. That bit you said was spot on. But I'm still doing it.'

He literally heard Jim take a deep breath for another attack. 'This shows weakness and...'

Thumb on speaker. Weakness? Now Jim would be trying to scare him with talk of myriad smaller gangs moving in to take what Fritz had left. They'd be thinking: the big baron had folded before a rival and handed him goodies on a plate, so for sure he'd do the same for others.

When the buzz ceased, Fritz said, 'Wow, I never thought of that. Smart man. Still happening.'

'The revenue from...'

Fritz didn't cover the speaker this time. He put the phone on the carpet and went into the bathroom to piss. When he returned, he heard Jim asking if he was still there.

'Sure. I was just speechless because you scared me so bad. Guess what? Changes nothing. And I'm selling all my legitimate businesses too. Everything's going, Jim. And then *I'm* going. You're the best in the business, so you'll be okay. Just tell Zander you need a job. He'll bite your hand off.'

Fritz hung up.

SEVENTY-THREE

Louis pulled into a service station on the A1 for some sleep just after 2am. He set an alarm for seven, but woke naturally five minutes before it went off.

He immediately thought of Sonia. Was she with the police? Were they trying to trace the phone he'd used? Was she distraught that he'd left and being consoled by officers? How were the kids coping with daddy's disappearance? Or was Sonia still asleep, as yet unaware that he'd abandoned her? Abandonment was sure how it felt, even though he was trying to save his family.

He told himself to stop. He couldn't think about any of it. Not until he'd been to the address listed for a man called Bruce Spence. Part of him hoped he'd find nothing but disappointment there and would have to return to Grimsby with his tail between his legs. He missed his family already.

But it was a small part of him. The rest wanted to move on with the plan, and fast.

He no longer trusted this car. It might be hunted. He couldn't steal a vehicle because it would be reported immediately. He chose to misappropriate the registration plates from a car parked in a Premier Inn next to the services. It would give him only a little extra time, but it might make the difference.

He bought tape and a screwdriver from a WHSmith in the services and committed his crime. After ordering food at a McDonald's drive-through, he hit the motorway again. His spirits were at rock bottom, but that was a good thing. When you were trapped at the bottom of a well, the only way was up, and every inch in that direction brought you closer to freedom.

He entered London around 10am. It wasn't a gated city, there was no obvious boundary, but he felt a change in the air. A rising of his anxiety. It felt like entering a designated danger zone. But the new fear in his belly spurred him on.

He was tempted to fly by his home and see if the building still stood. But he didn't want bad news. It would remind him of Sonia and the kids, and the task ahead required putting aside everything that mattered in his life. He also needed momentum in order to fuel determination, so he drove straight to Bruce Spence's address.

It was an end terrace on an impoverished street running parallel to train tracks, half a mile west of Parry Estate. He parked right outside.

The house looked grimy. The upstairs bedroom window was missing a pane and clear plastic had been used in its stead. The living room window had cardboard taped over a portion. The lawn was overgrown and littered. In the driveway was a car missing its wheel, bonnet and engine. Bruce Spence didn't have a working vehicle, then.

Actually, he did. Movement in his rear-view mirror showed Louis that a car had just pulled up behind him. A young, shabbily dressed man got out with a Tesco carrier bag and headed through the gate.

Louis moved fast. If he paused for thought at any time, he'd likely baulk. He followed the man up the path, unnoticed. The front door was unlocked. As the young man entered, Louis rushed him. He put his impetus behind a solid forearm thudded into the back of the man's neck. As the man stumbled forwards into the hallway, to crash into the bottom of bare wooden stairs, Louis stepped in and shut the door.

He kicked the man hard in the ass, then grabbed him round the back of the neck. He pressed the man's forehead hard against a stair nosing.

Just then came a thumping from a room above. Another young man appeared at the top of the stairs. He wore boxer shorts and nothing else. There was an Xbox controller in his hands.

'Who the fuck are you?' he yelled. He threw the controller, but it missed Louis and broke apart on the floor.

The biggest threat was the guy upstairs, so that was who got Louis's focus. 'You know who I am?'

The man upstairs made no move to come down. He'd lost some bravado now his missile hadn't dropped his enemy. 'No. Who are you?'

'You know my friends?'

'No, man, got no bloody clue. Why are you here?'

'Did I come here with a bag over my head?'

'We've done nothing, man. What do you want?'

'Bear that in mind, boys. You don't know me, you don't know who I know, and I didn't hide my face. And I have your address. So don't try any shit, okay? Which one of you is Bruce Spence?'

The man with his face pressed into the stairs responded. 'Just stop, mate, please. We don't want any trouble. He's not here. He's out. It ain't us.'

If true, that could be a problem, especially if this pair alerted

Spence. Louis couldn't leave. But he couldn't manhandle these two and certainly not a third. He needed a new method.

'Listen up, fellas. I need Bruce here, so one of you is going to call him. He's not going to get hurt. I need information. Now, I'm going to let you both go.' And he did. He released the fallen man's neck and stepped away until his back hit the door. The guy scrambled halfway up the stairs. The other guy came down to meet him.

'Don't try anything, fellas, because I have people who'll come looking for me. If you don't believe me, go right ahead and do your thing. But make sure I don't walk away from it, or I'll be back with a mob late one night.'

Neither man made a move. Louis knew he had them scared. He walked down the hallway. 'Follow me, lads. We'll wait in the living room. I take one sugar in my tea.'

SEVENTY-FOUR

Around the same time, Fritz parked his vehicle near a car that was burnt-out and appeared to have been destroyed some time ago. It, like the rest of the housing estate in Hackney, was a decrepit mess. There was trash and graffiti all over the place. Throngs of kids hung around everywhere he looked.

Little thugs like this, who rarely left the estate, wouldn't know who he was. The newspapers would have a field day if London's top criminal, untouchable by major organised crime groups, was killed by a gang of little fourteen-year-olds. He was a little worried.

The housing block was no better. Broken lift. Stairs that stank of piss and were an obstacle course of junk. The communal corridor on floor four had a wastewater pipe on the ceiling and nasty yellow shit had leaked and formed blobs and icicles.

He tried the door of number 19 and found it open. That was begging for trouble around here. He stepped inside. He'd never been here before, and for that was thankful. The flat was no cherry atop the cake. The hallway walls were covered with mould. All doors were open and he saw the same mould in the bathroom, living room, even the kitchen.

He stepped into the main bedroom at the end. Double bed with crumpled quilt. Tall wardrobe. Grimy curtains over the window. But in amongst it all was the gem. A wide table bearing a high-end computer with three monitors. Other electronic equipment was there, including a mound of mobile phones in a shoebox. Above it all was a wall-mounted TV featuring a gameshow, *Deal or No Deal*.

The aforementioned was all modern, but the man who owned it was not. Dressed in a crumpled T-shirt and tracksuit bottoms, he sat before the workstation in a cheap iron wheelchair. He was seventy-seven years old.

'All the money I give you and you live like this? In a council place?' The man wore a headset, so heard nothing. Fritz pulled it off the shiny dome of his bald head.

Jim turned. 'Ley. What are you doing here?'

'What's with all the mould? Bad for someone your age.'

'It's all over every flat. The council can't do anything. Why are you here?'

Fritz pointed at the TV. He knew the gameshow. A contestant picked one of twenty-two sealed boxes, all of which contained a written sum of money between 1p and £100,000. Blue boxes were low amounts, while red denoted higher sums. The contestant eliminated boxes over a number of rounds, while being given offers for his box by The Banker.

If the contestant liked an offer, he could deal. Offers would rise if blue boxes were eliminated since that increased the chance of the contestant's box containing a high sum, and vice versa. If the player no-dealt all the way to the end, he got to open his box and keep whatever was inside.

'I've had a good, long think about my past, my future, but

mainly my present. That show is a good analogy for my life,' Fritz said.

'Ley, talk to me. You never come here. I'm not sure I like it.'

Fritz ignored the question. His eyes were on the TV. 'I've been lucky. Every box I opened in my life was blue. Low amounts. Year after year, until I got left with all the important red boxes. Nothing but good things in them. Lucky me, right?'

Jim wheeled his chair backwards, to put extra distance between him and Fritz. 'Ley. I don't like this. You're angry about what I said. I didn't mean it.'

'The problem, Jim, is that I still had boxes to open. That's the game. But, when you're at the very top, down is the only route open. Nothing but red boxes to lose.'

Jim looked scared. There was sweat on his wrinkly brow. 'We found them, Ley. There's only one left and we'll get him. We'll soon have all the men who killed Sam. I'm helping you do that.'

Fritz forgot the TV and looked at him. 'I was too greedy. I chased greatness for too long. And, in the end, I lost the most important box. I wanted more, and more, and I got my boy snatched away from me because of it.'

Jim said nothing now. Perhaps he knew it was fruitless.

'I should have known when it was time to cut my losses. Now I do. No more boxes for me. It's time to deal. I'm getting away from everything, Jim. I'm turning my back on all of it.'

Jim opened his mouth, but he got no chance to speak. Fritz's hands clamped on his throat. And squeezed hard.

'Here's the thing, Jim. When you turn your back, that's when someone is most likely to stick a knife in it.'

SEVENTY-FIVE

Fritz didn't like how his wife seemed to jump between emotions, like a scratchy double-grooved vinyl record. But he realised he'd been acting the very same way. Sometimes he flipped grooves if he saw a young man who looked like Sam or a father with his son, which seemed appropriate.

But there was no discerning the full list of catalysts because earlier he'd stubbed his toe and flicked from angry to brooding in a nanosecond. On another occasion he'd hit that hidden groove because he got a scare when he opened a cupboard and a Pot Noodle fell out. It wasn't as if Pot Noodles had been his son's favourite food, which might have been enough to spark a dour mood.

Some sparks made more sense, though. He was driving east on the A2 and saw a sign for the Dartford Crossing. Immediately it put in his mind an image of Dartford Heath, where he and Marie and Sam, then six, had once visited on a Christmas afternoon.

He parked on the shoulder and got out. He retrieved an ice scraper. The edge of the heath was lined with tall, thick shrubbery, but he found a gap and passed through. Once down the embankment on the other side, he needed just seconds to find a path and moved north. A trek of four hundred metres led him to the car park, and from there he easily found the tree where, so many years ago, he'd hammered in a black nail at head height.

He took ten steps in the direction he needed and, close to a row of bushes, stabbed the ice scraper into the ground. It was a fragile tool, so he worked carefully. Visitors walked here and there, but nobody questioned what he was doing. It took him half an hour to dig eight inches down, at which point the scraper hit something solid.

Five minutes later, he hauled the metal box out. It was four inches by six and three deep. A button unlocked it and the rusted lid creaked open, but then broke free from decrepit hinges. No matter.

Inside, he found a plastic teddy-bear key-ring, a notebook full of Sam's doodles, and some plastic vampire teeth. Sam had put those in there. Other items, placed by Marie, included a bagged lock of Sam's hair, one of his lost teeth, and a pair of his first baby socks.

But Fritz concentrated on three other items. One was a small gun that looked real but was actually a lighter. A fake series E £20 note, which had gone out of circulation just a couple of years later. And a fake passport that he'd had made up in Sam's name.

He'd slipped these items into the box while Marie was back at the car to fetch something. He hadn't wanted her to see because she wouldn't have agreed. And of course not. What father would put such items into a time capsule? What kind of father would give his son a gun that looked real, or fake money, or a bogus passport?

And why had he liked these items so much? That one he knew the answer to. This was back in his heyday, when power and violence meant its most to him. Back when he glorified such things.

Back when he'd *wanted* Sam to follow in his footsteps.

Fritz felt his eyes well up. He snapped the toy gun in half and tore up the passport and the note, and scattered the pieces.

Well, he'd gotten his wish, hadn't he? His boy had trodden in his father's shoes, and now look. Marie had hinted at the truth, and so had a detective on the day this hell descended. Fritz hadn't killed his boy by failing to shield him from the badness orbiting the family. He hadn't been too weak or naïve to steer his boy onto a safer path.

No, he had pushed his boy directly into the face of danger. The conflicting emotions, the depressing thoughts, the lack of energy: nothing to do with grief. It was pure, unfiltered, 24-carat guilt.

SEVENTY-SIX

Louis couldn't stomach a cup of tea, but he wanted something to occupy his shaking hands. He also wanted a weapon, just in case.

It wasn't necessary. The two lads obviously ran in criminal circles. They might be mean. They might be tough. But they would know that real badboys were out there, people with serious connections, and they'd know an important safety rule of the streets: be careful who you piss off.

So they made him tea, and they sat together across the dingy room from him. They'd told him that Bruce was out on the rob, and that they weren't really his friends. He was someone they knew and he was homeless, so they'd let him crash at theirs for a few days. After that, they said nothing. They tried not to wilt under his glare by pretending the TV was interesting.

One of them had sent Bruce a text, which Louis had reviewed before it was dispatched. No warning. Just a note to hurry back and bring milk. Nineteen minutes after the text, the man of the hour was back. When they saw his pushbike pull up outside, the two lads offered to go wait in their rooms.

'Good plan. You ever met the Carter Crew?'

They shook their heads.

'You don't want to. Have no part in what happens down here, even if Bruce calls for help. Just stay hidden and I'll have no cause to mention your names to the wrong people.'

They nodded and made themselves scarce.

Bruce walked in. He yelled that he had milk. No one replied. Bruce then entered the living room, carrying the plastic bag. He saw Louis sitting on the armchair, gave a thumbs-up, and walked into the kitchen. Perhaps his friends had strangers over often.

Louis followed him and stood in the doorway as Bruce popped the milk in the fridge. He also had a satchel, probably loaded with stolen gear. 'Bruce?'

'Dudes call me Spotter.'

That hit Louis like a hammer. Spotter. He was one of The Ninja Warriors, tasked with making sure the police didn't surprise the gang. He wasn't sure if he should be angry with this guy or not. He also wasn't sure how much of the truth to tell him.

Spotter grabbed a banana from the fridge and sat at the table. He stopped in mid-peel, now aware that their guest hadn't stopped watching him. 'So who are you?'

Louis stepped fully into the kitchen and shut the door. A washing machine blocked the back door, which had no handle mechanism. No escape. 'Mr Fritz is after the men who killed his son. He's killed two of them. You know where number three is?'

Spotter sat up straight. 'Mr Fritz sent you? But he knows I–'

'Number three is in your kitchen right now.'

The lie felt terrible, but it got the desired effect. Spotter looked at the back door. He looked at the kitchen door. No escape. And then he looked at Louis. He was terrified. 'I'm just low-level scum. I'm no one. I had nothing to do with any killings.'

Louis believed it. However, he had nobody else. No other leads. Just this one straw to clutch at, which he did with another lie. 'I know exactly who you are. I'm here, after all. I want Fritz and I know you have good information. I want it. Be careful with lies. You don't know what I know about what you know.'

Spotter belonged to The Ninja Warriors, the gang run by Sam Fritz. Sam Fritz was Ley Fritz's son. Surely Spotter would have heard his leader utter a useful snippet of information at some point in history. The type of car his dad drove, a pub he drank at, a supermarket that delivered his groceries – anything that could push Louis even one fairy step closer to his target.

'I can give you Fritz's address,' Spotter said.

SEVENTY-SEVEN

Back home, Fritz called Marie's name. No answer. He headed upstairs to find the bedroom empty. The walk-in wardrobe was open and one side was empty. His side. He went to the window and looked out.

She was in the back yard, feeding flames down by the fish pond. She'd collected branches, but the bulk of the bonfire seemed to be clothing. His. He headed into his office, where he had a pristine The Who's *Tommy* 'Pinball Wizard' machine. No longer pristine. The glass had been smashed and the whole device flipped onto its side.

He opened one of the desk drawers, hunting his rock. According to his mother, he'd picked up a small white stone when he was just months old and never let it go. She had allowed him to keep it. At the age of five, he'd sworn to keep the stone in his possession for fifty years. He'd now had it for forty-nine of them. Gone.

Next he went to the spare bedroom, where he'd hung pictures of his mother and the father he barely knew. The frames were smashed, the pictures inside torn to shreds and scattered. That confirmed it. Marie had destroyed everything that mattered to him. He knew why.

These events hurt, and he was dearly angry with her, but none of it changed his plan. He hadn't just come here for a stone. He headed into the garden. She was watching the fire, her back to him. He said, 'Spring clean?'

She turned. He knew that face: simmering rage a half-second from the boil. But her voice was a tranquil pond. Unlike the actual pond, which was coated with paperwork. No doubt important stuff and all his.

'Jim called me while you were out,' she said. 'I'll give you three guesses what about?'

'I'll just take one. He said I was dumping the business. We both know Jim is always right.'

She breathed through her nose so fast her nostrils flared. 'You want to give everything we've worked hard for to one of your rivals. That's not happening. So get that straight. But I'd like to know what possessed you.'

We? She hadn't lifted a finger to help him build his empire. It had already been standing when she materialised. 'Call it colonic irrigation. I'm starting over. It's something you need to do, too.'

She laughed. 'Oh yes. You want to get away from London. Start a fresh, new, law-abiding life. Such a sweet idea.'

He took a deep breath. The vital moment. Possibly a big mistake. But he spoke the words he'd practised and dreaded. 'And you can come with me.'

'What?'

'I caused all this, Marie. Too much pain and too much spilled blood. And not just Sam's death, but you, too. You're not right in the head, but it wasn't always that way. You're a warped psycho, and I never would have gotten with a woman like that. That means you changed. And I changed you.'

She sneered at him. 'These are the words that you hope will convince me to ride into the sunset with you?'

'Just honesty. Right now I don't want you. You treat me like something you stepped in. You're a timebomb. But there's a chance that, if we get away from this lifestyle, you can go back to being the woman I fell in love with. I was ready to leave, but guilt got me about you. It seems only right that I try to fix what I caused. The truth is, I hope you'll say no, but I'll offer you that chance. Right now, you and me, away we go to restart and see what comes of it.'

'I'm not going anywhere with you. How foolish are you?'

His tense shoulders relaxed. 'Then please have a good life, Marie. Where's my white stone?'

'Piss off.'

He turned to leave. She followed, firing insults at his back. He walked through the kitchen and got to the doorway, where he stopped as she said, 'You lost this time. Jim and I will run the business. We've already discussed it. We've already told Zander Bajaj he's getting nothing.'

He turned. She was in the back doorway, filling it. The bright world beyond her meant he couldn't really see her face. But he knew she was smiling.

'I know, Marie. Zander called me. He said Jim was plotting against me.'

If that worried her, he couldn't see it because her face was in shadow. 'You're not fit to run anything anymore,' she said. It was a barely more than a whisper, but it hit him like a scream. 'You lost your mind. You lost what made you great.'

'What I lost was my son, Marie.'

She bared her teeth: he saw that much. 'So did I, you bastard. Because of you, just like you said. But unlike you, I didn't curl up in a ball and decide to wither away in the dark.'

'No, this is the opposite of dark. I saw the light, Marie. It showed me that I can still have a happy life, and I don't need power and money and blood for it. I don't need revenge to honour Sam's soul.'

She laughed around her sneer, which was a very ugly expression. 'You bought me this house, so don't you go thinking you can sell it. It's mine. I'll move Jim in. This will be where we'll run the business f–'

'Jim's moving nowhere but a cemetery.'

She paused, letting this news sink in. 'You killed him?'

'Suicide. He plotted against me.'

She burst into a speed he didn't know her big body was capable of. In a flash, she was at a worktop, where she snatched up that goddamned receipts spike, as if determined to have a head on it after all. Before he really believed it was happening, she charged at him.

SEVENTY-EIGHT

Kilton Park, home of Ley Fritz.

Louis drove along a quiet road that looked like it belonged out in a Peak District village. He passed a single shop and moved alongside the tree-shrouded fence surrounding the exclusive gated enclave. Large homes were visible here and there where the woods were thinner.

On his right, a little further down, was the entrance to the private community, which he'd already seen the layout of on Google Maps. The security hut was a flat octagonal building with windows giving a panoramic view, and exposing the single guard inside like a museum exhibit.

He drove past and parked around a bend. On the internet, he'd found the website of the Kilton Residents' Association, which maintained the communal grounds.

Boasting about their fabulous slice of the world, the KRA had mentioned that CCTV cameras were dotted along the perimeter fence and disguised as tree branches. There were four gates, each alarmed. Security personnel manned the main entrance 24/7 and regularly patrolled the grounds with dogs, although privacy was in no way compromised.

Oh, and three chart-topping singers and a movie star lived there. No mention of the capital city's biggest criminal also having a residence, though.

Louis had an idea. He abandoned a dangerous plan to climb a tree, hop the fence, and scuttle amongst shadows.

Step one: check local news for mentions of Kilton Park. He got a hit. Four weeks ago an export magnate had thrown a party that his neighbours had deemed too loud – but that was it. No stories of bomb attacks. No knifeman found lurking in bushes. Not even a stalker hassling someone famous. Bizarrely, no incidents of dawn raids by police, either. Somehow Fritz had avoided such a thing.

Step two: find a home for sale. He entered the website of an estate agents called Bustwell's, which featured a Kilton Park mansion called Green Vale. It was £4,550,000. Wow. It had once been owned by a man the description referred to as a 'biotechnology firm CEO'. Maybe he was involved in bread production and enjoyed a fancy title. Or he was a pharmaceutical director who hated being called a drug dealer.

Final step: get inside. Louis drove back to the gate and turned into the driveway. There was an intercom, but the guard unglued his eyes from a TV and came to the window. He was probably thankful for human contact. He certainly didn't look at his visitor with suspicion.

Louis said, 'My name is Mr Jones and I'm here to view Green Vale for a client. Call a company called Samson Logistics and ask for a man called Smith. He'll transfer you to Mr White, who will email you a copy of my identity card. Then please call Bustwell's, which is the estate agent, who will confirm the appointment. Their representative will be along to meet me in half an hour. Please hurry up.'

The moment of truth. Kilton Park wasn't a place where trouble visited. The guard had probably security-checked dozens of people, all ultimately legit. He could go through all the hassle Louis suggested, or he could assume everything was kosher and get back to his TV.

The gate started to retract.

Louis drove inside and turned left. He passed the first massive house, took a right, and thirty seconds later came across the expansive home of Ley Fritz. Didn't someone once say crime doesn't pay? He spotted at least three security cameras just watching the front of the property, so sneaking round the back to jimmy a window a no-go.

Sod it. He pulled up and got out. Went straight to the front door and knocked.

No answer. No sounds from inside the house. Only one other home was visible from the doorstep, and there was nobody around. He tried the door, and it opened. People trusted guard dogs, it seemed. He stepped inside without pause.

So far, this had all unfolded surprisingly easy, and it had an air of fate about it. He was destined to finish this here, or he was not. He had not once considered that Fritz might be armed, or surrounded by goons. Louis's body seemed to be out of his control, his mind nothing more than a passenger taking a ride and half-asleep because of it.

Was that autopilot from his army training? A mental breakdown? Blind panic? A death wish? He knew only that he would not, could not, stop to think about the consequences of confronting London's most powerful crime magnate in his lair. So he pushed on. Momentum for determination.

He walked through a hall, and in its centre stopped dead. Doors lined the walls and beyond one that was wide open was a large kitchen. Inside, on the floor, in a pool of blood, was a body.

SEVENTY-NINE

It wasn't Fritz lying dead. It was a big woman in a nightie. It must be his wife, named as Marie in a newspaper story that had called her a chubby barmaid.

Louis wasn't the only man hunting the crime lord. He ran from the room, looking in others. But with caution now, for her killer could still be in the property. Fritz had surely been the main target, and he could be dead in another room.

Every room on the ground floor was neat and clean, no sign of a robbery. Valuables everywhere. There was a security office, but whoever worked there was gone. Also dead somewhere? Or had Fritz's protectors turned on him and his wife?

Upstairs, every room was as pristine as those below, except one. In an office, a pinball machine had been smashed and tipped over. Sometimes burglars had a specific target – was the game a secret hiding spot that the attackers had known about? Had Fritz hidden important documents there?

Fritz wasn't in the house. Louis looked out a back window onto a long lawn where a fire was dwindling. Had Fritz burned evidence? Mid-afternoon was a strange time for a bonfire. Had the killer of his wife started it?

It was all very puzzling, but also pointless to dwell over. He was here for Fritz, and Fritz was gone. Louis headed downstairs, to leave. In the hall, he glanced again at the kitchen.

The body had moved slightly.

Louis approached her. The woman still lay on her back, but her arms were in different positions. As if to dispel his confusion as to her state of life, she blinked up at him.

'Who are you?' she wheezed. Closer than before, he noticed the blood was pooled mostly around her fat legs, which were dotted with stab holes. A bloodied kitchen knife was nearby. 'Here to kill him?'

He grabbed tea towels from a rack and bent over her, examining the wounds, pressing the towels against them, and telling her to stay calm, promising that help was coming. The blood flow had slowed down. It was a strange collection of wounds. Who targeted only the legs?

'He's gone,' she said, her voice weaker. 'Sicko is with boyfriend. Thinks I don't know. Always known. Mind is gone. You the man he calls Ghost?'

She had information, but he didn't care. The knife might have hit vital veins and she could bleed to death. Kneeling by her, he pulled out his phone and dialled 999. She reached up and tried to grab the device, but there was no strength to do other than stroke it before her hand thumped to the linoleum.

'Him and his man,' she croaked. 'Am I so ugly I turned him off women?'

'Don't talk,' he said as he lodged a tea towel under her head and wiped hair from her eyes. The call was answered. He described the scene, gave its location, and hung up.

He'd ordered her to not talk, but she disobeyed him. She wheezed four words, and then closed her eyes and breathed out for the final time.

EIGHTY

'I'm sorry, baby.'

'Where are you, Louis? Where did you get all that money?'

Autopilot seemed to have switched itself off after he'd left Fritz's mansion. With time to let his mind breathe, Sonia had filled his thoughts. He knew where he was and what he was doing – but she had none of that information and would be worried sick. He had to call her.

'I can't tell you where I am yet. I'll be back soon. The money is from Newton. I didn't know how to tell you. Are you with the police?'

He imagined officers in the room with her, instructing her on what to say. Maybe they had told her what kind of trouble he was in, and that it was in his best interest to surrender. And she had to make him do it.

But she said, 'No. I can't do it without you, Louis. I don't want to sit with them on my own. You're part of this. I want you here. I'm still in the hotel with the kids. I think you left that money because you are worried you won't come back. But please come back, right now.'

'I can't. Not yet.'

She started crying. 'Don't do this. I know what you're doing. We'll be safe, Louis. I looked into the law on joint enterprise. It was reassessed a few years ago. Now a court has to believe that you assisted or encouraged Owen to kill that boy. I don't think you'll go to prison for murder. We can get through this.'

She sounded choked with emotion, but it only heightened his desire to find Fritz, do... *something*, and make her and his children safe. 'I'm nearly done, Sonia. I'll be back with you before long.'

'No, Louis, you'll be back now. Don't do something stupid. Don't do something that will get you put in prison.'

Was that his plan? To do something stupid? He had no clue, did he? He was barrelling towards a scenario – facing down Fritz – but had no idea how things would play out thereafter. What would he do? Convince the man to leave him alone? Kill him?

His mind was fuzzy, faulty, misfiring. It threw up an old saying: *It's better to be judged by twelve rather than carried by six.* It felt like the voice of someone else. Sonia on one side, that voice on another, both of them battling for command of him. And he was stuck in the middle, unsure of his next move. Had he called to reassure her he was okay, or to seek her help in halting his forward action?

Fritz will kill everyone you love if you don't stop him.

'Louis? Are you listening? Please don't do this. I'm begging.'

He'll never stop hunting you and your family.

'Hand yourself in Louis. We can be protected. Please.'

Fritz has connections and the police won't be able to save you.

'Come home, Louis,' Sonia yelled.

'I can't yet. I love you, Sonia. You and the kids. I have to do this. I'll be back, I promise. When it's over.'

'Do you want to speak to Louise and Theo? They miss their dad.'

Just hearing their names put a lump in his throat. He had known men in the army who'd refused to call home for fear of derailing their will to battle on. Others had needed the emotional support from loved ones. He wasn't sure which side he was on until he made the decision.

'No.'

If he heard even one syllable of sound from Louise or Theo, he'd fall apart. If they begged for his return, he'd end it right here. He'd abandon his plan, scuttle back to his family, and surround them with a danger he could have stopped but didn't.

'Tell them I love them. And Daddy will be home soon. Save that money just in case.'

He hung up. He broke apart the phone and lobbed it out the car window.

Two opposing voices had vied for his commitment, but the future had already been decided by a third hours earlier. By the final four words Marie Fritz ever spoke:

'Farmhouse. Minster Leas beach.'

Louis stared through the windscreen, across a field rippled by small hills and shallow depressions. At a farmhouse overlooking the beach.

EIGHTY-ONE

The sun would be setting soon and, although it would offer cover, Louis did not want to do this in the dark. He left his car in a pub car park, where he'd been for an hour. He crossed the hill road, climbed a fence, and dropped into a field. Half a mile north to the farmhouse. The land was uneven, and in the low portions he lost sight of the building. Here he would pause for a moment, as if he needed his target in view to be magnetically connected to his mission.

A hundred metres out, he paused again, this time with the farmhouse dead in his sights. If he was worried about being visible out in the open, a sound eroded that fear. A terrible screech that carried across the land. It sounded like a saw. Like someone was doing DIY inside the building. The noise would cover his approach. That person – Fritz? – would have his attention elsewhere.

He moved quicker and covered the final metres in a sprint. Just like at Fritz's mansion, he did not delay in case he baulked. He tried the front door and it opened. That air of fate blew across him again.

He shut the door and walked down a hallway, past a flight of stairs, and peered into the first room. A living room. No one there. Next, a lounge, also free of people. Bathroom. Lifeless. These rooms got only a cursory glance, for his objective was the door at the end of the hallway, from behind which came the noise of the saw.

He opened it fast. A kitchen. It was in the mid-stages of renovation. A dust sheet covered the floor and the worktops had been removed. Busted wood and tools were everywhere. The replacement worktops were in flat-pack form against one wall. There was a topless man on his knees, using a power saw to wet-cut tiles. His back was to Louis. Behind him was a four-socket extension reel into which the tool was plugged.

This man was young, big, muscled, and he had long hair in a bun. Not Fritz. The boyfriend Marie had mentioned.

The man must have had a moment of confusion as the blade of his saw stopped, yet a wailing racket continued to fill the kitchen. Then he turned, and he understood the scene. His tool had been unplugged. His orbital sander had been connected instead and now whirred in an intruder's hands.

'Where's Fritz?' Louis yelled over the din.

'He thought you might come,' the man shouted back. 'Let's call him Ley, please. I'm Josh. And you must be the one he calls the Ghost.'

EIGHTY-TWO

The words of the man called Josh disarmed Louis. Literally. He turned off the sander. 'What do you mean, he thought I would come?'

'He said he made mistakes. He let you know you were in his crosshairs. You got one over on some men, so that proved you have skills. And you're an ex-commando. He said a man like that would probably come after him. And here you are. Are you the one who killed his son?'

'Where is he?'

'Are you going to kill him? He thinks you might. Weirdly, though, he told me to tell you exactly where he is. Despite that.'

Louis lowered the sander. This was going far from how he'd imagined and it was throwing him off. 'And where is that?'

Josh was still holding his saw. He put it down. 'I'd rather you didn't kill him. We're setting up here together. It's been a long time coming. But, anyway, he gave me an order, so I'll do what he wants. I had to send him away because he'd get under my feet while I was working. But he also said he didn't want to talk to you here. Follow me upstairs.'

Josh moved towards Louis. Louis stepped aside, holding the sander between them, finger on the trigger. 'He's upstairs?'

'No. Just follow.'

This was all so bizarre that Louis didn't trust or distrust the man. His brain didn't offer an option for an action, so he went with the only one provided: follow. He felt drunk.

They headed up the stairs, into a bedroom at the back of the property. Louis kept his distance, just in case of a blitz attack, but that meant Josh had a few seconds alone in the bedroom.

And when Louis carefully entered, he found Josh standing before the window. Facing him across the bed. Aiming a bolt-action blue rifle with a telescopic sight right at his chest. Behind Josh, at the window, were a tripod and chair.

'I love Ley and I want nothing more than to pull this trigger. It's loaded. I can hit a bird a hundred metres away.'

Louis had never come across this weapon, but he knew it was a Russian Snow Wolf SV98, and it was accurate at ten times the aforementioned distance. He put his hands up. 'Maybe I don't plan to kill Fritz.'

'I'd love to be sure, and this would help me guarantee it. I know he killed your friends. But he wants to talk to you, so I can't.'

Josh turned and placed the rifle on its tripod, barrel aimed at the closed window. He sat on the chair and put his eye to the scope and moved the gun slightly, as if searching for something. Louis could see part of the field, Marine Parade, the beach, and beyond it all the North Sea.

'I don't actually shoot. Ley does that. Hates the seagulls. One divebombed him as a kid, nearly took an eye. I just watch the eye candy. Here.'

Josh moved away from the rifle. He wanted Louis to try it. The man could have put a hole in his chest twenty seconds ago, so Louis doubted this was a trick to get the upper hand. He passed the bed and approached the gun.

He sat and put his eye to the scope. It had a simple dot reticule. Filling his view was a portion of the beach and the sea, easily two hundred metres away but magnified to appear as if the farmhouse was right on the edge of the sand. There was a haziness on the left side of the lens because of the setting sun.

It was early evening on a cold day and the beach wasn't busy. Only one man was in the scope. Wearing jeans and a trench coat, he had his back to Louis as he threw stones into the water. The hair matched a photograph he'd seen.

Fritz.

Louis felt his heart thud, which caused the dot reticule to waver. He slowed his breathing, as he'd been taught so long ago, and the dot settled. On Fritz's head. It would be so easy to–

'Don't,' Josh said. 'You came for him because he's killed your friends. Imagine what I'll do if you take away my soul mate.'

Louis stood up. Without a word, he left the room. Josh followed him downstairs, and to the front door. Here the young man paused. 'Don't do anything stupid,' he said. 'I'll be watching. I think you know what I mean.'

Louis stepped into the field. And walked towards the beach. Ten metres into that journey, he turned and looked up at the bedroom containing the sniper rifle. The window was now open.

Yes, he knew what Josh had meant by *I'll be watching.*

EIGHTY-THREE

The sea was painted orange by the setting sun, which under any other circumstances would have been a beautiful sight. The tall man on the beach seemed to be enjoying it. Louis felt the scene had an ominous aura.

He walked across the sand, towards the man. He didn't feel fear now, nor anger. A void filled him. There were a handful of people around, strolling with lovers or walking dogs, but nobody within range of hearing Louis's shout: 'Fritz.'

Fritz turned slowly, no surprise, as if he knew his enemy stood there. They were thirty feet apart. 'Thank you for what you did for my wife.'

How did he know? Louis figured it was the CCTV cameras in his home – like Newton, Fritz must have mobile phone access to their feed. 'You watched her die?'

'In a sense. I saw her after she was gone. I saw the police there, just an hour or so ago. I saw the body. I rewound the video and watched you arrive. I watched you try to help. I didn't kill her. She came at me with that knife, but I disarmed her and left. She did it to herself. I had to watch that, too.'

'I know you didn't do it. I could tell by the wounds. But it's another death in a life full of them for you.'

He nodded. 'And it will end with my own. Hopefully not for years to come. I'm sorry to say you won't get the chance to be the one. Josh is watching.'

Louis knew it. The killing dot was probably on his head right now. 'I'm not even sure that was my plan. I still have no idea why I came here. I'm not like you.'

'I don't think I'm like me anymore. Come closer, you're safe. Let's play.'

Play? It was soon clear what Fritz meant. He used the heel of his shoe to draw a four-line grid. Nine squares. Noughts and crosses. He put an X in the middle. He waited. Louis remained where he was, now just ten feet away. 'No games.'

Fritz picked up a white stone from the beach and twirled it in his hands. 'Owen Moore. I wanted to kill him personally. I wanted to slice him, beat him, and make sure he looked into my eyes when he died. But he was tortured for information he didn't give, and he got taken from me.'

Dormant anger rose in Louis. He kept it leashed. He wondered if it was better that Owen had avoided this bastard's hands.

Fritz drew a o in the sand for Louis 'That doorman, Allen, who had nothing to do with this. But I didn't know it at the time he was killed. By then I'd lost the urge to get hands-on. I wanted his murder on video. That felt like a good second-prize. But he was killed by accident.'

'Bullshit.'

'Have I a reason to lie? Sure, I would have had him killed, but I didn't. Accident.'

Louis couldn't hold the anger in check, but nor could he forget the sniper rifle aimed at his skull. He settled for a verbal assault. 'You're an evil bastard, Fritz. I hope there's a hell. If not, one should be created just for you.'

Fritz carved his X into the beach. 'With Newton Meecham, I barely cared anymore. Not even about a video. I just wanted him gone. A man pretended to fix a car, and put a knife in his neck.'

Louis said nothing this time.

Still playing with the white stone in his hands, Fritz said, 'What I felt after that was incompleteness. A job not yet done. One more man. The ghost. You.'

Louis almost felt the weight of Josh's eye on him through the rifle scope. Had this all been a trick so Fritz could watch Louis die right before him?

'But it wasn't that kind of emptiness,' Fritz continued. 'It was the loss of my son. Still there. Always there. The killings didn't help. They were like... plasters on a decapitated head. What's one more plaster going to do? There's no point. If I'm to find peace, it needs to be some other way.'

Louis had to repeat Fritz's words in his head to make sure they registered. Was the man saying he didn't want another kill? That Louis could live?

As if reading his mind, Fritz drew a second o for Louis and said, 'I don't want to kill you, Ghost. Not you, not anyone else. Ever again. I wanted you here so I could know which of you actually killed my son. But I don't even care now. In fact, I don't want to know–'

'Owen Moore,' Louis cut in. 'So you got your man on the first try. The others were innocent murders.'

'Actually, none of you killed him. The reason my boy is dead can be traced much farther back. To a brash young father who thought it would be cool to bring his son into his lifestyle.'

Fritz had marked his last X, but he'd missed a chance for three in a line and left the win for Louis. He didn't want to play stupid games, but he saw a chance to take something, no matter how tiny, away from this man. He stepped forward and turned his foot in the sand to create a ○. Drew a line through it. Kicked the board into nothing. Stepped back.

Fritz stared down at the mess. 'I'm getting out, Ghost. Away from everything. That's why I'm here. It might not last. But I need to try. A rival is stepping up to take my place. Got your phone? Google my son. Do it now.'

Louis would not take orders from this man, sniper rifle or not, but he knew... something had changed. So he pulled out his phone and made the search.

At the top of the first results page was a news report from earlier that day. An arrest made in the murder of Sam Fritz, son of notorious villain Ley Fritz. He read it with growing astonishment. Mark Hinds, a gangster who went by the nickname The Hammer and was currently serving a life sentence, had admitted to arranging the murder, as well as other killings. Those of all the players in this fiasco.

Louis felt his legs go weak. 'I don't understand. Who the hell is Mark Hinds?'

'I made mistakes,' Fritz said. 'Those killings would come back at me when they got tied to my son. I had to give away almost everything, but with the last of my influence, I've managed to shift the blame away from all of us. I now just want peace and solitude. None of you will be in the frame for my son. It's best if you know none of the finer details.'

Louis couldn't get his head around it. He saw a speck light at the end of the tunnel, but it was hazy and he didn't dare run for it. The best he could do was seek confirmation of a gut feeling. 'I'm...free?'

'The three of you dressed as ninjas to take on The Ninja Warriors. People paid you. People know. The police will soon know, and they'll come for you. But on that night Owen Moore didn't kill my son. By a quirk of coincidence, someone else was already targeting him that night. Did you see the killer?'

'What? No. I mean, I don't understand what–'

'He thought you did. The man who killed my son thought those three ninjas saw him and could tell the police. So he chose to wipe out those witnesses. Anyway, that's finer detail territory, and I said something about finer details, didn't I?'

Louis took a deep breath of sea air and waited a moment. There was a settling in his mind, and it was enough for him to understand at least one thing. Again he said, 'So I'm free?'

'Like I said, the police will come. Tell them almost everything about your plan. You'll be fine. You and your people killed no one.'

Louis didn't miss the words *almost everything*. 'But I can't tell the police about you, right?'

'Nothing you can say will wreck the cover story that's been set in place, even if you mention such a cover story. All you have is conjecture, while the police will have evidence effectively refuting all that you think you know. You can't hurt me.'

It wasn't lost on Louis that he'd twice asked a question that had been ignored. For the third time he said, Louis, 'So I'm free?'

'Did you come here for revenge, or to make your family safe?'

He wanted Ley Fritz to burn in hell, but he hadn't been fuelled by vengeance. 'I don't want my wife or children to be hurt, or to live in fear. That's all I want. I don't even know how I planned to achieve that.'

'Then you have no desire to come back some other day to take your pound of flesh. Do you burn with guilt that your little escapade resulted in the death of a boy?'

If asked that question even ten minutes ago, he would have screamed *no* to hurt this man. He couldn't do it. Seeing Fritz before him had changed something. Evil or not, the crimelord had lost a child, and Louis couldn't imagine the pain. Perhaps, in Fritz's position, he would have also sought to severely punish those responsible.

But he also felt compelled to utter the truth. 'No. And not because of who he was. I didn't know him. I didn't kill him. Moore tricked us. I would have stopped him if I'd known.'

'Then you have no reason to tell the truth and say my name or this location.'

'As long as I lie to the police and I don't come for you again, you won't hurt me or my family? Is that what you mean?'

Fritz licked a finger and cleaned the white stone in his hands. 'I had a stone like this for almost fifty years. Maybe I can keep this one just as long. What's your name?'

Louis could have lied. It wouldn't have increased his chances of remaining safe, though. He spoke his full name.

'Louis Cooke, you can't hurt me by what you do or what you say. But I don't want to look over my shoulder ever again, not even once. If you try coming for my blood, or you speak my name, then we'll have further business. But I think we won't. So go home, Louis. If I haven't miscalculated something, we can both enjoy a long life.'

Louis didn't move. Like his wife before him, he had researched joint enterprise and believed there was a chance he could avoid a murder charge if he came clean. But there would be a price to pay if he told the police the truth. He could walk now, and he could have his kids and wife back, and be under no threat, but he would have to live a terrible lie.

He was at a fork in the road, unsure which route to take. He would have preferred a single lane, no choice to make, destination already determined. But that part of the story was for another time and right now he wanted to close this chapter by riding into the sunset.

Yet still his feet wouldn't move, and he now knew it wasn't indecision that froze him to the spot. It was fear. This man had killed Louis's friends and targeted him, and he just couldn't accept that it was now all over so easily. Surely there was a trick afoot. It seemed preposterous that this man would have a sudden change of heart and let go free a man who might have killed his son.

Yet it seemed to be. Fritz turned away and stared across the sea, or into the sky, which looked as if God had spilled tins of paint. So Louis turned away, aimed at the road, and set his feet moving.

And stopped as he caught a glint from way in the distance. Past the sand, the tarmac, the grass. From the farmhouse. Sunlight glancing off glass. Off the lens of a rifle scope. He tensed. A trick after all.

He heard the faint crack of a high-powered round being loosed.

EIGHTY-FOUR

There was no second shot, even though the first had missed him. Louis knew he should run, but the training that he'd assumed was dormant was once more.

He couldn't force his legs to start moving.

He saw no more glint of sun on glass, but he did spot movement. A tiny speck in the gloom, moving away from the farmhouse.

A second.

A third.

In total, five men fled the building. One by one, they crested a rise and vanished behind it.

Seconds later, he heard meaty engines that sounded like motorbikes or quad bikes. He saw nothing, though. Not even headlights. And soon that sound faded.

Only then did he turn around, and he saw what he expected. Fritz lay face-down in the sand, blood leaking from a shattered head. The white stone he'd planned to keep sat in the wetness, bright against it.

The silence was rent by screaming. Others on the beach were now aware.

Their cries awoke logic in him. He understood. Fritz had miscalculated something after all. And now there was no fork in the road, just a single lane dead straight into the inevitable.

THE END

A NOTE FROM THE PUBLISHER

Thank you for reading this book. If you enjoyed it please do consider leaving a review on Amazon to help others find it too.

We hate typos. All of our books have been rigorously edited and proofread, but sometimes mistakes do slip through. If you have spotted a typo, please do let us know and we can get it amended within hours.

info@bloodhoundbooks.com

Printed in Great Britain
by Amazon

62067484R00160